The Pattern of Piney Series

HOOKED
by Love

BOOK ONE

By Katharine E. Hamilton

ISBN-13: 979-8-9856240-1-4

Hooked by Love
The Pattern of Piney Series
Book One

www.katharinehamilton.com

Cover Design by Kerry Prater.

This is a work of fiction. Names, characters, places,
and incidents are either the product of the
author's imagination or are used factiously, and
any resemblance to actual persons, living or dead,
business establishments, events or locales is
entirely coincidental.

"The family–that dear octopus from whose tentacles we never quite escape, nor, in our inmost hearts, ever quite wish to."
Dodie Smith

All Titles
By Katharine E. Hamilton

The Brothers of Hastings Ranch Series
Graham
Calvin
Philip
Lawrence
Hayes
Clint
Seth

The Siblings O'Rifcan Series
Claron
Riley
Layla
Chloe
Murphy
Sidna

The Lighthearted Collection
Chicago's Best
Montgomery House
Beautiful Fury
Blind Date
McCarthy Road
Heart's Love

The Unfading Lands Series
The Unfading Lands
Darkness Divided
Redemption Rising

A Love For All Seasons Series
Summer's Catch
Autumn's Fall

Mary & Bright: A Sweet Christmas Romance

Captain Cornfield and Diamondy the Bad Guy Series
Great Diamond Heist, Book One
The Dino Egg Disaster, Book Two

The Adventurous Life of Laura Bell
Susie At Your Service
Sissy and Kat

«CHAPTER ONE»

"I'm sobbing. My face is pouring tears—"

"Don't you mean your eyes?"

"What?"

"Your eyes. Don't you mean your eyes were pouring tears? How can your face pour tears, when tears come from your eyes?"

"You're missing the point. Okay, fine, my *eyes* were pouring tears, my nose was all drippy and slimy, and I'm pretty sure I drooled on myself as I belted out the words to 'All Out of Love' by Air Supply. Heart-wrenching. Devastated."

"Dramatic?"

"Hey now, I was sixteen and Tom Felton had just shattered my innocent heart."

"Mom, first off, Tom Felton is an actor on Harry Potter, not your first boyfriend. If I remember correctly from the last two times you've told me this story, his name was Todd Franklin. Second, Air Supply? Really? They're not even from your generation. Let's be real here, you were probably crying to a Backstreet Boys or NSYNC song."

"What? How dare you? I liked the classics."

"Riiiiight."

"Look, I'm just trying to have an open conversation with you about why it is important for you to steer clear of boys at your age. Sure, they have those neat little hipster haircuts and button-up shirts that for some reason they wear two sizes too small, but hey, I get it... they're cute and charming. But boys are trouble. They say sweet things, maybe even give you a little pet name after a while, and then when you least expect it... BAM! You're sixteen, in the hospital, alone, delivering a baby and having to face the hard truths of this world by yourself, haunted, thinking, 'I should have listened to my mother.'"

"Mom?"

"What?"

"We're talking about me right now, not about what happened to you."

"Oh, right... well, you get the picture. Boys bad, mom rules, and you're too young to have a boyfriend." Reesa Tate tapped her fingers on the edge of her steering wheel as she nervously glanced at her daughter. "Clare?"

"Yeah?"

"You get it right? Where I'm coming from?"

Sighing, bored with the topic and her mother's stories, Clare nodded as she crossed her arms over her middle. "But you get it too, right? That I'm not you?"

The burn of that comment pelted her in the chest, but Reesa nodded. "I do. You're smarter than I ever was, that's for sure. Maybe not as cool—"

"Mooom!" Clare glanced her direction in offense and Reesa laughed.

"I'm kidding! Geez, kids can't take a joke these days. So sensitive."

"You also realize that I have no chance at a boyfriend right now anyway, right? And that this entire conversation was pointless."

"A conversation with my daughter is never pointless," Reesa countered. "I always have a point to make. It may take me a while to get there, or I might make several different points along the way, but all conversations with me have a smidgen of value... even if it's just for the entertainment." Clare rolled her eyes at her mom's lame attempt at complimenting herself. "And why so negative all of a sudden? You were just telling me about all the cute guys in your class, and now you're saying no to the boys?"

"Ummm... because we're moving." Clare waved her hand at the road in front of them, the early morning darkened highway only visible within a few feet of headlight range as the sun slowly began to rise. "Like, literally moving right now, I doubt I will fall in love on my first day at a new school next week. So no, no boys in my future any time soon."

"Oh my lanta, what if you did fall in love your first week of school?" Reesa gasped. "Oh no, I'd be heartbroken. What would I do? You'd ditch me and I wouldn't have anyone to eat corn chips and ice cream with!"

Clare's lips twitched, and Reesa knew she'd achieved her ultimate goal of relaxing her daughter as they headed toward their new life in Piney, Arkansas. This move had been spur-of-the-moment, as were most of their moves over the years, but Clare had taken it all in stride. Their belongings were tucked neatly away in the small, rented travel trailer hooked up to the back of her beat up SUV. Reesa had no problem moving; she actually liked changing places every couple of years. She'd never quite felt settled anywhere since she left home at sixteen. She'd worked hard to give Clare a safe, fun, and adventurous lifestyle, and as they headed to their new home, which she could have sworn they were about to reach, she hoped this move would be even better than the last.

"How much further?" Clare leaned her head back against the headrest and glanced over at her mother's slightly confused expression. "We're lost, aren't we?"

"No. No, we are not. It's just tricky."

"Tricky?"

"That's what the woman said. I am directly quoting her. Oh!" She sharply turned the wheel to the left and they bounced to high heaven on an unforeseen pothole. "Oh Lord, tell me that wasn't a body." Reesa gripped the wheel as they continued to bump their way down a dense, tree-lined dirt road.

"Mom, I love you..." Clare began, leaning forward in her seat to peer up through the window at the tunnel of tall trees. "But where in the world are you taking us?"

"A quiet, pristine cabin in the woods," Reesa quoted from the house listing.

"Ummm..." Clare nervously glanced at her mom.

"It said it was charming," Reesa muttered, as they reached a small clearing and a weather-worn cabin stood before them. The sagging roof and off-set front door held little promise as she parked behind a sporty black luxury SUV.

"Well, that's at least a little comforting."

Reesa turned off the car and glanced at Clare. "Coming?"

"Nope." Clare waved her on. "One of us has to live should something bad happen."

Unbuckling her seatbelt, Reesa climbed out. "Drama queen." She shut her door and paused at the slanted concrete steps leading to the wide-planked front porch of the cabin. The screen door squeaked open, and a wire-framed woman stepped out in hot pink capris and ostentatious floral top. Her lips matched her pants, and, to Reesa's impressed surprise, her fingernails.

"You must be Reesa!" The woman embraced her and squeezed both her hands. "Honey, you are gorgeous. Welcome to Piney. I'm Billy Lou, your new friend, tour guide, and landlord." She laughed at her own comment and patted Reesa's shoulder. "Now, where's that daughter you told me about?" She looked over Reesa's shoulder and waved for Clare to step out of the car. "Poor thing looks scared to death. I promise I don't bite."

"She's just a little nervous about the move."

"Of course, anyone would be." Clare stepped out of the car and hesitantly closed the door. "Hey, darlin', don't be scared. Come on now," Billy Lou greeted Clare warmly, sizing her up and then looking Reesa over again. "Yes, you two will do just heavenly for these parts. Come on in." She waved them into the cabin, and the floor creaked under their feet.

Reesa felt Clare slide her fingers in hers and she squeezed her daughter's hand in reassurance.

"Now, I know it doesn't look like much, but lots of great memories have been made here in this little house." Billy Lou pointed to the small open-concept layout of the living room and kitchen. A small wooden table, that slanted heavily to the left, was tucked to the side of the kitchen with three chairs. A scraping noise had all the women jumping until a figure began climbing to its feet behind the table. "Theodore James Whitley, you scared me to death!" Billy Lou held a hand to her heart and then smiled lovingly at the looming man before them. Reesa's eyes traveled from the worn-out work boots up the long, faded jeans to the filthy, work-stained t-shirt that hugged a proud chest and beefy build. The broad shoulders straightened at Billy Lou's comment, but the overgrown bearded man did not appear apologetic.

"Grandma. Sink's fixed."

"Oh, wonderful!" Billy Lou clapped her hands together. "Reesa this is Theodore. My grandson. He's my mister fix-it for anything and everything." She lovingly patted his arm and then nodded towards Reesa in a silent 'be polite' motion. Theo extended his hand.

"Theo or T.J," He corrected his grandmother as he introduced him.

"Reesa Tate. This is my daughter, Clare."

Clare's eyes widened at being brought into the conversation, clear fear of their potential living situation evident on her face.

"Nice to meet you," he grumbled. "I'm done here, I believe." He looked to his grandmother, and she gave a firm nod. "Reesa and Clare have moved all the way from Connecticut. Isn't that somethin'?"

Theo grunted as he tossed his tools back into a dented red toolbox that looked to be either a second-hand find or a family heirloom. Billy Lou pointed to a small pink paper taped to the freezer door of a 1950's GE refrigerator. "I have his number and mine written on there for you, should you need anything. The landline works fine, her hot pink nail pointing to an ancient rotary phone on the kitchen counter. Now, I can't guarantee you'll always have cell phone service out here, but should you need anything, you have a way to reach us." She smiled as she pointed to Theo. "Why don't you start unloading their trailer, honey."

"Oh, no, that's not necessary." Reesa waved away the offer. "We'll be fine."

"You sure, darlin'?" Billy Lou asked. "I'd hate for you girls to be luggin' heavy furniture by yourselves."

"We'll be fine," Reesa assured her. "We've had lots of practice."

"Very well." Billy Lou narrowed her eyes at Theo as if to say, 'you help anyway' before she walked towards the door. "The water valve is outside by the woodpile, should you need it. Just watch for snakes. And the breaker box is in the closet of the room down the hall on the left. The fuses are sensitive in this old house, so you'll become familiar with that box. Just give them all a flip every now and then. I think it gives it a little reset that just keeps things runnin' smoothly."

"Great." Reesa thanked Billy Lou as they all walked towards the porch once again and the older woman turned with a wide smile.

"Happy to have you two here. I hope you are able to get comfortable and acquainted with our little town. And it's just a short hop over to Hot Springs should you need to go to Wal-Mart or the grocery store. My house is about three miles that-a-way." She waved to the east through the forest of thick pine trees, only a few feet visible past the tree line. Theodore is that way." She pointed to the west side of the woods. "Cemetery is a mile or two behind ya." She pointed to the back of the cabin. "Not much out here, but it's peaceful, and town has all kinds of fun activities, shops, and good eatin' spots. Might take you some time to get situated, but everyone is already excited to have some new blood in town." She grinned and reached to give Reesa another welcoming hug that doused her in Estee Lauder perfume. "I'll check on you girls in a couple days to see how you're settlin' in, but if you need me before then, you just give me a holler, okay?"

"Thank you, Billy Lou." Reesa smiled in thanks as the older woman climbed into her sleek vehicle. She gave a final wave before driving off.

Theo stood awkwardly on the bottom step of the porch. "Sure you don't need any help?"

"I think we're okay, thanks."

He grabbed the heavy toolbox, nodded a farewell to them and began walking, and looked to be paving his own path through the trees in the direction of his house.

"Strange man barreling through the woods? Not creepy at all," Clare murmured. "Where have you brought us, Mom?"

Reesa began humming the tune to Deliverance, and Clare shoved her. "Not cool, Mom. Not cool."

"Come on, it's not that bad. With a little Tate girl flare, this place could be really cute."

"Tate girl flare? This place needs a complete overhaul. Do we even have hot water?"

"You know, I didn't ask." Reesa pondered that a minute and then shrugged. "Guess we will have to see. Come on, let's start unloading." She walked to the back of the trailer and lifted the loading door. "Which room do you want?"

"Does it matter?" Clare asked.

"Not really. But go pick which one and I'll take whatever you don't want."

Clare grabbed two boxes with her name marked on the side, climbed the creaking porch, and disappeared into the small house. Reesa watched her go and then palmed her face in her hands. Where in the world had she brought them?

~

Theo watched a moment through the trees just to make sure there wasn't any overly heavy furniture he needed to assist with. He saw the basics and loads of boxes, but nothing that seemed to be pressing for a little extra muscle. Good. He was ready to be home. He'd worked a full day at the shop, and he was exhausted. The last thing he wanted to do was help two city girls unload a trailer. A scream had him turning back towards the cabin and he dropped his toolbox and ran. He cleared the trees in a leap as laughter spilled through the air and the woman stood at the base of the trailer with an avalanche of boxes around her feet and on top of her. Her daughter, flushed from sprinting from the house, noticed him at the edge of the woods and rushed towards her mother as he walked forward as well.

"You okay?"

Reesa climbed to her feet and dusted herself off, pausing when she noticed Theo.

"I heard a scream." Her shoulders relaxed a smidgen, but he realized how creepy he must seem, having disappeared into the woods and reappeared in a blink of an eye. He could tell he'd scared the teenager.

"I'm fine. Sorry for worrying you." Reesa brushed her dark hair out of her eyes. "I was never really great at Tetris."

He didn't say a word, and she fumbled at what to say next.

"Or Atari in general. Before my time. But I was killer at Paperboy on Nintendo. That little dog never stood a chance. I—"

"Mom." The girl cut her mother off from babbling and Reesa cleared her throat.

"Right. Well, thanks for coming to the rescue."

"No problem." Theo nodded towards the couch. "Sure you don't want help with that?"

"We got it." Reesa nodded for Clare to climb into the trailer and grab the opposite end of the small loveseat.

He gave a firm nod of the head and headed back the way he'd come.

"Such a creeper." Clare commented, quickly receiving a harsh shush from her mother. He cringed on his way back through the tree line. Whatever. They didn't know him or the ways of this town. He was neighborly. He heard a scream, so he came to help. That was kind. Not creepy. He stooped to pick up his toolbox on the trail through the trees and the short trek brought him to the backside of his house, an excited bark awaiting him. He set his tools down as his spunky black lab, Trooper, came barreling towards him. The dog excitedly jumped into his arms and licked his chin, the wild brute never growing out of the puppy phase as was promised by all who 'knew dogs.' That was all right though. Theo loved the crazy lunatic anyway, and the two of them had a quiet and uneventful life in Piney. Well, until Trooper escaped the fenced yard and dug up all of Billy Lou's spring tulips last year. The dog had been blacklisted as a town nuisance ever since. But Theo didn't mind. It meant people left them alone for the most part. He worked in town at his mechanic shop, came home, cooked supper, watched television or read a book, and then repeated everything the next day. Life was slow-paced in Piney, and he liked it that way. Trooper, however, needed excitement every now and then, so Theo planned to take the dog to the pond the next morning and let him swim while he fished; their typical Saturday adventure. He walked into the house, Trooper hot on his heels as he grabbed a cold beer from his fridge and walked back outside. He grabbed a small metal pail off his deck and walked to his small garden patch and began picking green beans. The spring crop always did well this time of year, and he was drowning in beans thanks to the small fence he'd placed around his garden to keep the deer out. He handed a bean to Trooper and the lab laid on his belly in the dirt and munched while Theo worked. He heard the phone ringing inside the house, and he set his bucket down and made his way there. On the fourth ring he answered. "This is Theo."

"Theodore," His grandmother's voice carried through the phone. "I'm at the salon. Marcie needs a jump; that old heap of hers is actin' up on her. Can you come?"
"Be there in a few."

"You're a sweet one, honey. Thank you." She hung up and he whistled for Trooper, the dog jumping to his feet and sprinting towards him.

"Load up." Trooper jumped in excitement and Theo laughed. "Yeah, yeah, yeah, you get to go to town. Don't make a fool out of yourself." He opened the tailgate of his truck and Trooper jumped in, giving a lick to Theo's ear as he walked along the side to his door. "Cheap shot." He swiped a hand over his slimed ear and grinned as he got behind the wheel and headed towards town.

He arrived in less than ten minutes to the quaint little shop tucked amongst Main Street's historical buildings. The bright turquoise painted brick was still a bit over-the-top, in his opinion, but the salon was all the local ladies had without having to drive into Hot Springs. And Meredith, the main hairdresser, wasn't too shabby with a pair of scissors, therefore her little shop was always buzzing with activity. Theo climbed out of his truck and pointed at Trooper. "Stay." The dog whined. "Stay," he repeated, and headed inside. He ducked beneath the shorter door frame and stepped inside, the dainty bell on the door tinkering as he walked in. "There he is! My hero!" Marcie Lowens, his second-grade teacher, beamed up at him as he nodded his greeting to the various women in the building. "Good to see you, T.J." She patted his shoulder. "Thank you for coming to help me."

"No problem, Mrs. Lowens."

"I love a man with manners." Betty Hoke, one of the many ladies his grandmother played bridge with once a month, batted her eyelashes at him.

"His momma and daddy raised him right." Billy Lou walked up and patted his cheek. "Sorry to call you away from the house, darlin'."

"Not a problem. I'll get Mrs. Lowens' car going." He walked back outside and popped the hood of his own truck to run jumper cables over to the small car next to his. He knew he had an audience; he felt all eyes on him as he worked.

"He datin' anyone, Billy Lou?" Betty asked.

"Why? You interested?" Billy Lou teased on a laugh.

"Just wonderin'. I knew you said he had a girl a few years ago, but he's not married, so I'm assuming that didn't work out."

"No, poor thing. That girl ripped his heart up and spit it out. Cheated on him."

The women gasped in unison.

"And he hasn't dated since?" Meredith asked, as she clipped strands of Shirley Denison's dyed blonde hair.

"Not really. If he has, I haven't heard about it." Billy Lou watched as her grandson reached into Marcie's car and the hood of her car popped open.

"Not right for a man to be alone." Betty shook her head in disappointment.

"Don't be hard on my boy," Billy Lou defended. "He can be alone if he wants to."

"It's not right, Billy Lou, and that's a fact. It's Biblical. Look it up."

"Oh, posh." Billy Lou rolled her eyes. "The good Lord may say that in His holy word, but if He wants that to be the case, then he needs to provide a good woman for the boy. He has yet to do that, so I'd say that it's partially on the great I Am's shoulders."

Theo cranked the engine and Marcie's car sputtered to life for what he hoped wasn't the last time. He unhooked his cables and rolled them up, neatly tucking them back into his toolbox on the back of his truck. He rubbed a hand over Trooper's head before walking back towards the salon. The ladies, indiscreetly, hurried away from the windows. The bell jingled as he poked his head in the door. "All is well, Mrs. Lowens. But you need to have that battery replaced soon."

"I'll get on it, T.J., thank you."

"Theo," Betty Hoke waved him inside, "I was just curious," she began. "I have a niece over in Hot Springs, about your age, single... would you be interested in meeting her?"

His face blanched. He hated this question. He hated being put on the spot. And he hated meddling. His eyes darted over towards his grandmother, and she clapped her hands to break the silence. "Now,

Betty, I told you, Theodore is very happy with his life just the way it is. Thanks for comin', sugar. On your way home, could you check on our new arrivals? Make sure they're doin' alright?"

"Yes ma'am." He palmed a brief farewell to the rest of the women and hurried towards his truck.

"New arrivals?" Betty asked.

"We're rentin' out our old fishin' cabin to a young mom and daughter who just moved here from Connecticut."

"Really?" Intrigued, Shirley waved away Meredith's hands from her head and turned in the salon chair to look at Billy Lou. "You turned down my daughter two months ago, but you have a stranger moving into this town and rented it to her?" Her tone hardened and Billy Lou's chin slightly raised.

"That's right."

"Billy Lou Whitley, how incredibly rude," Shirley snarled.

"Not so. Your daughter has torn up the last two houses she's lived in, Shirley. It's no secret. Forgive me for not wanting that to happen to my property. Besides, this young lady and her daughter needed a place, and the Lord put them in my path. I wasn't about to go against the Lord's calling." She narrowed her gaze to see if Shirley challenged her. Shirley pursed her lips and turned back to face the mirror.

"What's she like?" Betty asked. "The woman?"

"Oh, such a charming girl. Beautiful. Her daughter looks to be about fifteen or so and looks just like her mother. That's about all I know."

"A complete stranger," Shirley muttered, shaking her head in dismay.

"This town needs some new blood," Marcie Lowens chimed in. "Especially amongst the younger folks. I look forward to meeting them, Billy Lou. Invite her to bridge."

"I will, Marcie. I think that'd be a lovely idea."

"Well, I look forward to meeting her too." Meredith swept the cape from Shirley's shoulders. Meredith, a divorcee in her early forties, had been the youngest single female in town for over four years; no doubt she looked to have some of that pressure taken off her shoulders.

A bark sounded from outside as a screech and clash sounded. The women bolted outside as Theo stepped from his truck in a hurry to the car he'd backed into, and Reesa Tate stepped out.

CHAPTER TWO

"*You okay?*" *Reesa reached* across the armrest to Clare and her daughter nodded. "Fine." Though the passenger door was slightly dented inward towards Clare's side. Reesa placed a calming hand to her heart as she saw Theodore Whitley rushing towards her door. He yanked it open and all but lifted her from her seat.

"You hurt? Everybody okay? I'm so sorry."

She gripped his elbows, his firm grip on hers as well as his dark eyes roamed over her face. "I didn't see you guys. I was... lost in thought. I'm so sorry." He peeked into the car and saw the dented door and Clare's ashen face. "Oh God. He leaned into the car and Clare turned wide eyes his direction as he asked her if she was hurt.

Reesa walked to the passenger door, but it wouldn't budge. She yanked several times and it did not move. It was then she saw her daughter clamping a firm grip on Theo's forearms as he helped her climb over the center console and out the driver's side. She stood on shaky legs and Reesa walked over and enveloped her in a tight hug, both women shaky. A tongue licked up her bare leg and she jumped before looking down at the black dog at her feet. He sat, his soulful eyes pouring into hers as if he felt personally responsible for his owner's transgression. She melted to her knees, as did Clare, as they hugged the dog and rubbed behind his ears and spoke in soothing tones. "What a sweet boy you are." She let him lick her nose and chin as he turned and did the same to Clare, his back leg thumping as Clare found his sweet spot on his ribs and tickled him. The teenager giggled as Reesa stood to her feet.

"You sure you two are okay?"

"Fine. It wasn't a hard hit, just looks like it was." She pointed to her car.

"What are you doing in town?" he asked, then realizing it sounded absolutely inappropriate, changed his tactic. "I mean, you guys still had a lot to unpack."

"We were starving. Thought we'd come to see if there was a local pizza joint or diner or something before tackling the rest."

Billy Lou hurried down the steps of the salon, her hair freshly fluffed and curled. "Reesa, honey." She embraced Reesa firmly against her in a quick hug. "You girls okay?"

"We are just fine, Billy Lou. Thanks."

Billy Lou hit Theo on the shoulder with force and she shook her finger at him. "Theodore, you know better than to just back out without lookin'. You could have killed somebody."

"Honestly, we are fine." Reesa tried to smooth her feathers and flashed Theo an apologetic look as his grandmother continued to scold him. His expression was grim, or at least what she could tell from behind his bushy beard.

"You will fix her car for free, Theodore James. You hear me?" Billy Lou continued. "FREE."

"Oh, that won't be necessary. I'm sure my insurance will cover it. And I'll find a local mechanic to—" Billy Lou pointed at Theo. "Oh, you're the local mechanic."

Theo nodded.

"Well, that works out then. Saves me time hunting one down." Reesa looked down at the dog and her daughter. "Cute dog."

"Thanks."
Billy Lou's eyes darted between them before she reached for Reesa's hand. "Honey, how about I take Clare to go get a bite to eat over at Seymore's," She pointed up the street. "While Theo gets your car over to his shop. You two can meet us over there. Then after, Theo, you will drive over to Hot Springs and pick up some groceries for the girls. I placed an online order while I waited to get my hair done. There's nothing in that cabin, and I know they'll be completely worn out from moving before they even think about the store."

"Oh, you didn't have to do that." Reesa didn't quite know what to do with the current information.

"I know. I wanted to. And I'm glad I did now that my grandson caused such hardship."

Did he blush? Reesa's eyes landed on Theo's features briefly before glancing down at Clare. "You alright with that, Clare?"

"Sure." She stood to her feet, the dog nudging her fingers as he sat beside her.

"Come on, sweetie." Billy Lou motioned for Clare to follow her. "We'll see you in a few." She draped her arm over Clare's shoulders and began chatting away as she walked onto the sidewalk and led the way.

"I'm... sorry about this, and her." Theo waved the direction of his grandmother.

"Don't be. She's great." Reesa nodded towards her car. "So, what do I do?"

"I can tow it, but I think it will run just fine if you just want to follow me to my garage."

"Okay." She slid behind the wheel and looked up at him. He jolted to attention and walked back towards his truck, his dog hopping obediently inside the cab this time. His garage was just up the street. T.J.'s Automotive, the sign read in big blue letters, the paint chipped and peeling as if he hadn't bothered updating the building or signage in over a decade. He climbed out of his truck, and she watched as his long legs walked to one of the far bays and he lifted the metal roll up door and motioned for her to pull her car inside. She shifted into park and turned off the engine. Grabbing her purse, she climbed out. "Well, that it?"

"For now. I'll give it a good look over tomorrow morning and then we can talk about what needs to be done."

"Fine with me." She shut the door on a sigh and shouldered her purse.

"Hungry?"

"Starving like a hostage." She grimaced at her comment. "Not meaning I *feel* like a hostage, just... never mind. Yes. I'm hungry. I hit starving about an hour ago. It hasn't been pretty. I ate a breath mint to tide me over. It was gross. It was in the bottom of my purse. Had fuzz on it. But, hey, desperate times call for desperate measures, right?"

His brows scrunched as he listened to her ramble on, and she forced a smile. "So, food?"

"Right." He pointed to his truck. "Climb in." The dog sat between them and occasionally snuck a lick at either Theo's ear or Reesa's cheek.

"So have you lived here your entire life?"

"Most of it."

"Your parents live here?"

"They're over in Hot Springs."

"Nice." Reesa reached into her purse and fished out her wallet, thumbing through the cash; she had to make sure she could cover her supper if the place didn't accept credit cards. She tucked it back into her purse. "The school pretty decent?"

He eyed her curiously. "It was when I went there, but that was a long time ago."

"How long? You look about my age, but I can't quite tell with your beard which, by the way, is very Charles Darwin-esque. Bet that took a long time to grow. Be careful though, you're on that borderline of turning Tom Hanks Castaway if you're not careful."

Ignoring her beard commentary, he replied. "Fourteen years ago."

"Been a while, then. My daughter will start Monday at the high school. She's a sophomore."

He didn't respond and she drummed her fingers on her knees. "Your grandmother seems nice. I'm glad. My last landlord was a nightmare, so this should be a nice change of pace. Clare was terrified of the man. Guess we both were, really. He sort of had this Cruikshank vibe to him. What's even worse is that we lived on Mockingbird Lane. Weird, right?" He smirked and she continued. "So, when I saw a cabin in the piney woods of Arkansas, I thought, hmmm, this has to be better. Done."

"That's how you made your choice? Just picked a place?"

"Yep. That's how we do it."

"Then this isn't the first time you've moved across country?"

"No. It's sort of our thing."

"Is that not hard on your daughter? So many different schools?"

"Not really. Clare's a pro, and she's awesome so she makes friends easily wherever we go. Oh look, a dentist office. I need to go there at some point. I've had this weird pain on one of my molars for like a year." He parked his truck in front of one of the old storefronts and led the way through a swinging glass door, the smell of fried food breathing life into her lungs. She spotted Clare up ahead laughing at the story Billy Lou was telling with hand flourishes and animated gestures. "There they are." She walked towards the table and smiled, Billy Lou scooting over for Theo as Reesa slid in next to Clare. He didn't sit.

"Everything sorted?" Billy Lou asked.

"I think so." Reesa smiled up at him, her face puzzling over his hovering.

"Theodore, are you not going to sit?"

"I'll go ahead and get to Hot Springs to pick up the groceries."

"No sir, you won't." His grandmother patted the seat next to her. "Didn't I tell you he'd try to escape me?" She looked to Clare for confirmation of her prediction. "You will eat the burger I already ordered for you." She pointed over his shoulder as the waitress walked up holding two plates of food. "Clare ordered for you, Reesa, I hope that was okay."

"More than." Reesa beamed as the plate of fried chicken tenders, French fries, and cole slaw was slid in front of her. She started to ask for something else when the waitress set two small plastic containers of ranch dressing by her plate. "You know me too well." She grinned at Clare as a massive burger was slid in front of Theo. "Wow, that's impressive. Good luck with that."

"He's a big boy, he can handle it." Billy Lou winked at the girls as Theo placed his napkin in his lap.

"So, Clare," Reesa looked to her daughter and tilted her head towards Theo. "He went to the high school here back in the day."

"Really?" Clare asked.

"Oh yes, he did." Billy Lou smiled proudly. "He was quite the athlete too."

"Interesting…" Reesa popped a French fry in her mouth. "He failed to tell me that."

"It was a long time ago, so there was nothing to tell." Theo shot his grandmother a warning look.

"If you walk by the trophy case next to the office, you'll see a picture of Theodore with his baseball team. They went to state his senior year."

"Very cool." Clare smiled. "What position did you play?"
"Pitcher." He took a sip of his drink and went back to eating, avoiding Reesa's curious stare. She wondered why he didn't brag. Didn't guys normally like being known for their athletic prowess?

"He had a full ride offer to University of Arkansas," Billy Lou bragged.

"You played college ball?" Reesa asked.

"No." Theo took a bite of his burger and the topic fell flat to the table like a lead balloon.

"When will the car be fixed?" Clare asked, looking to Theo.

"Not sure yet. I'll know tomorrow for you."

"In the meantime, I have a spare car you can use," Billy Lou offered. "It just sits in my garage covered up."

"Gran—" Theo began, his tone in shock at her suggestion. He paused in his outburst at her determined expression.

"That car needs to breathe, Theodore. And it does me no good just sittin' there. Someone might as well get some use out of it. And you won't use it or take it, so there." Billy Lou smiled at Reesa. "We'll swing by the house on the way to the cabin and I'll let you drive it back. Feel free to use it until Theo's done with yours, sweetie."
"That is so thoughtful, Billy Lou. Thank you."

"Don't mention it. You girls finished? We can head on over and take care of that. Theo, you go grab their groceries from Hot Springs and we'll meet you at the cabin." She stood and motioned for everyone to follow. "Theresa, put it on my tab, will you? My purse is in the car. I'll swing by tomorrow and take care of it." The waitress nodded and began clearing their plates.

Reesa stepped outside, linking elbows with Clare as Billy Lou whispered in hushed tones to Theo on her way out. "What do you think she's telling him?"

Clare grinned at her mom. "See woman. Nice woman. You man. You nice man to nice woman." Clare spoke in a gruff caveman tone and Reesa snorted in laughter.

Theo glanced up, his serious expression silencing both of them as he walked to his truck. Trooper greeted him with enthusiasm when he tucked himself inside and backed out of the parking lot.

"Come on, girls." Billy Lou waved them over to her SUV. "Climb on in."

~

So much for his Saturday. He knew the day's events were out of anyone's control, but he still wished he'd had his relaxing day of fishing. Instead, he pulled up the dirt road to the family cabin and felt his heart rate drum faster and his temper flare. There in the driveway sat his grandfather's prized 1966 Chevrolet Corvette in fire engine red. Polished to a gleam. He hopped out of his truck and started to pound his way to the porch when Reesa stepped out of the cabin, holding her finger to her lips, and rushing towards him. She grabbed his arm and turned him quickly back to his truck. "What are you doing?" he asked, his tone harsh.

"You have to convince her to take this car back." Reesa's eyes were wide with horror as she spoke in rushed and hushed tones. "There's no way I can drive this thing. It's-It's- It's... wow! And I'm... not. This is too much."

"Why didn't you just tell her no?" he asked, crossing his arms over his chest.

She leaned back in offense at his change in attitude and placed her hands on her hips. "Ummm, I did. But she wouldn't take no for an answer. And though I'd like to come clean and say I did thoroughly enjoy driving it over here, to feel that silky steering wheel under my fingers and the thrust of that gear shift that was soooo smooth—" She shuddered at the memory. "Wow. But I can't accept such an offer. I will mess it up. I know I will. And then I will feel absolutely horrible."

"My grandmother is hard to sway when she has her mind made up."

"But you can convince her. Just scowl at her. You've got that look down and it's somewhat intimidating. Trust me, I do *not* need to drive this car. I'm a distracted driver. I eat and crumbs fall between my thighs and just gets stuck there until I get out. I use greasy fingers to change the radio stations. I even make silly faces against the windows when I drop Clare off at school. Mouth prints on a '67 Chevy Corvette is and will not be acceptable. *I'm* not acceptable half the time. You have to help meeeeee—hey!" Reesa turned at the sound of Billy Lou coming out of the house, Clare tight on her heels. "Billy Lou." She smiled and then turned panicked, pleading eyes towards Theo.

"I've got the groceries." He motioned towards his truck and Clare walked towards it with him. Trooper hopped out as soon as he opened the door and made his way into the cabin as if familiar with the place.

"Whoa." Clare looked at all the bags. "Is there enough room for all of this stuff?"

"My grandmother believes in a stocked pantry."

"She clearly doesn't know my mother." Clare held up a can of beans in question.

"Whatever you don't want, just set on the back porch and I'll collect it."

"Oh, I didn't mean to sound ungrateful, it's just... my mom doesn't really cook... and this is all ingredients and stuff."

"She'll figure it out, I'm sure."

"Doubt it." Clare's muffled reply was hidden behind Billy Lou and Reesa discussing the use of the car again.

He was surprised Reesa put up such a fight. Anyone would dream to drive such a car, but he also liked that she wasn't willing to take such advantage of his grandmother's kindness.

"Honestly, Billy Lou, it's gorgeous. I'm pretty sure it hasn't stopped smiling at me since I drove it over here, but I'm too smart to fall for such a pretty face so quickly."

"Are you?" Clare asked in jest as she walked by her arms laden with grocery sacks.

Billy Lou hooted at the comment and waved her hand. "Honey, you are up the creek without a paddle. I'm offering you a paddle."

"Yeah, but you're offering me a rose wood paddle when a simple pine would suffice. It's too much. I can't accept."

"And how would you expect to get to work? Or to take Clare to school?"

"I work from home... most days," Reesa explained. "And Clare can take the bus."

"The bus doesn't come this far out, sweetie," Billy Lou challenged.

"Grandma, she isn't comfortable driving a stranger's rare and expensive vehicle."

Billy Lou looked them both over and tapped her chin with the shiny pink nail of her forefinger. "Fine. She'll use your truck and you drive it for the week."

"What?" they said in unison.

"Honestly, we'll be fine. It's not a far walk to town and I shouldn't need anything for the next several days." Reesa looked to Theo. "Which will give time for my car to be fixed, and before you know it, I'll be back on the road. Right?"

"Right." Theo nodded.

"I don't like it. Two young women out here in the woods without a means of transportation. What if something happened? An emergency or somethin'?"

"Then I'd call you." Reesa could see that answer did not cut it and then motioned towards the man looming beside her. "Or... Theo," she added in an uncertain voice, relaxing in relief when he assented to her suggestion.

"Goodness gracious, fine. Alright. I'll take it back and shove it back under its cover. It was just nice to let it breathe a bit."

"It's beautiful," Reesa complimented.

"My late husband treasured that car, so much so he put it above many other things." Her tone held a slight touch of bitterness. "No matter now." She forced her usual smile back to her face. "You girls get settled. We'll get out of your hair and let you finish unpacking."

Clare walked out of the house playfully tapping Trooper's nose as he jumped beside her. She giggled and ruffled his ears.

"You leave that dog with them tonight, Theodore," Billy Lou recommended. "Help them ease into the house."

"That would be fun." Clare looked up, her innocent smile erasing his immediate dismissal of the idea. He didn't like the idea of not having Trooper with him, but if it helped them settle in with a bit of canine security their first night, he'd suck up his own grumbling and let it be.

"That's fine. He sleeps inside. Hope that's not a problem."

Reesa shrugged. "Fine with me. Thanks."

"Alright, I'll leave now. You girls are exhausted, and not only do you have your belongings to finish unloading, but I added groceries on top of it. I'll let you get after it. Theodore, I'll see you tomorrow."

She hugged Reesa and then Clare before heading to her SUV. "I'll come get this monstrosity tomorrow." She pointed to the stunning Corvette with disdain before driving away.

"Well, I hope I didn't offend her." Reesa motioned towards the car.

"You didn't." He shut his truck door and knelt in front of his dog. "You stay here, Trooper. Got it?" Trooper licked his beard trying to reach his chin. "Yeah, yeah, yeah." He rubbed the pup's head and stood. "If you need anything, let me know. I live closer than my grandmother."

"Could you—" Clare interrupted with a finger. "Maybe check to see if the water heater is turned on?" She narrowed her eyes at her mom.

"I told you I would." Reesa held up her hands.

"I just washed my hands, and the water is freezing."

"Well, I've been busy," Reesa defended. "Teenagers." She rolled her eyes and then looked at Theo. "Do you mind?"

"No problem." He walked into the house and towards the utility closet, quietly taking note of the mattresses resting on the floor in the back bedroom and the half-unpacked boxes. He didn't spot any blankets or bedding and knew they must still have boxes in the trailer. What did they plan to sleep with tonight? Not his problem, he reminded himself. He adjusted the water heater and walked back into the living room, where Reesa was digging in a plastic tote.

"I don't know, Clare. Just use a towel tonight."

"A towel? I'm not using a towel."

"Well, I found one of those, it's the best I've got to offer." Reesa held up an old and tattered towel, two small trinkets unrolling out of it which she caught with speed before they hit the ground.

"It's going to be full of dust."

"It's only been in the bin a few days. It can't gather dust in just a few days." Reesa reached in the tub to fish around once more.

"Did you dust all the figurines and thingamajigs before packing them?"

Reesa looked dumbfounded. "Why would I do that?"

"Exactly." Clare shook her head in dismay. "Dust."
"Water heater should be good to go in about thirty minutes or so." Theo's eyes darted to the couch that was halfway in the front doorway and on the

porch, the screen door propped back on its hinges. "Need help with the couch?"

"No, that's all right. We just abandoned ship to look for sheets and blankets. I can't remember where I packed them."

Trapped inside due to the crooked couch jammed in the doorframe, Theo awkwardly stood in the middle of the room and watched as both women dug through box after box. Clare tossed another box to the side, a stack of books by her feet. Trooper sat patiently by her side, but his eyes held worry at all the commotion.

"I have some blankets you could borrow for the night," Theo offered. "Won't take me long to grab them."

"We have blankets," Reesa muttered, her annoyance growing as she held up a broken Darth Vadar bobble head. "Another broken one. What gives?" She growled and tossed it towards a trash bag hung on the back of one of the small dining chairs. It missed its mark and landed on the floor, the small clash of plastic on wood snapping Clare's head up from her next box.

"We have to call defeat, Mom."

"I see in your eyes the same fear that would take the heart of me..." Reesa paused for dramatic effect. "A day may come when the courage of men fails, when we forsake our friends and break all bonds of fellowship—"

"Mom!" Clare yelled for her to stop, the teen's exhaustion clear. "Stop quoting Lord of the Rings and accept his offer. I'm tired and I'm done."

Reesa set the box she'd been unpacking to the side. "Did you find your clothes?"

"Some of them. I already have them in the room."

"Why don't you try to hunt down your shampoo and by the time you find it, the water will be heated and ready. I'll go with Theo to get blankets for tonight."

"Thank you." Clare trudged towards her room, pausing at the edge of the short hallway. "Mr. Theo, thanks."

He nodded grimly as she snapped her fingers and Trooper hopped happily to his feet to follow her as if he'd been living with her the last few years instead of him.

"I'll fetch the blankets and bring them back if you'll help me move the couch." Theo pointed to his roadblock and Reesa palmed her forehead.

"Right. You can't get out of the house." She climbed onto the couch.

"What are you doing?" Theo asked, watching her slip and flop ungracefully across the sofa to the other side and out onto the porch.

"Grabbing this side. You grab that side." They lifted and tilted, the couch sliding free of its awkward position and carried it towards the double windows on the far wall and set it down. The old floral sofa had seen better days, the cushions worn, saggy, and faded. He didn't comment and Reesa didn't seem to mind the state of it. "Thanks."

"I'll be back." Theo hurried to his house through the woods, the half mile trek easy for his long stride. He loaded up a several blankets and two sets of sheets. From what it had looked like, both beds were queen sized and he had extra sets that would fit. He tried to think of anything else that might be helpful, but his mind was a blur. He grabbed the laundry basket laden with linens and headed back through the woods. He walked up as Reesa attempted carrying a wingback chair by herself up the porch steps. She stumbled at the top, but found her footing and he watched her make it through the door. Did she expect to unload the rest of the trailer by herself?

She spotted him when she came back outside. "Perfect timing. Clare just found her pillows. I think I wore her out with the drive and well... everything else today."

"I imagine so. I can help you." He motioned towards the trailer. "It won't take long to finish unloading everything."

Uncertainty flashed across her face as she reached for the laundry basket. "You don't have to. I can—"

"Handle it. Got it. And I'm sure you can, but I'm offering, and there's still a few hours of daylight left. With help, you could have it all unloaded by tonight."

Clare poked her head out the door and smiled at the bedding. "Thank you!" She took the basket from her mom. "I'm taking a shower and then going straight to bed. Don't expect to see me until tomorrow morning."

Reesa saluted her as Clare disappeared back inside.

"I guess my help has officially retired. You're hired."

He walked to the trailer and began unloading the larger pieces of furniture he could carry on his own as Reesa continued unloading box after box. Within an hour, the trailer was completely unloaded, and the small living room of the cabin was stacked and covered in boxes of all shapes and sizes. "And now I feel overwhelmed." Reesa sat on the old couch and ran her hands through her hair. "Where do I even start?"

"The kitchen," Theo suggested.

"Really? Why?"

"You asked, I gave an answer."

She grunted in amusement. "Are you always so matter of fact?"

"Most of the time."

She walked to the kitchen and rummaged through the pile of pantry goods stacked on the counter from the grocery sacks Clare had partially unpacked earlier. She found a bag of ground coffee. "I have a coffee maker in one of these boxes. If I'm going to unpack all this, I better caffeinate."

"I'll leave." Theo stepped over boxes and navigated his way to the front door. "If there's anything you need, write it down." He pointed to a notepad with magnet back hanging on the refrigerator door. "I'll check in on you tomorrow and will fetch whatever you need."

"Wow." Reesa leaned against the door as he walked down the steps towards his truck. "Is everyone in Piney as kind as you and your grandmother?"

"For the most part." He nodded a final farewell as he began backing out of the drive and slowly making his way up the dirt drive back towards the main road where he'd drive a half mile and then turn off onto a different dirt path that would lead to his house. It'd be quiet without Trooper, but he was so tired, he decided to be like Clare and call it an early evening. He had a feeling that tomorrow wasn't going to be any quieter, and for some reason felt that Reesa was just incapable of quiet. Period. The woman was odd. She talked constantly, and she seemed scatter-brained most of the time. He had to admit she was nice to look at though; dark hair and eyes and a pretty smile. She also had a nice figure. Curvy and— he interrupted his own thoughts with a harsh scolding. No. He couldn't think along those lines. She was new in town and off limits. Plus, she had a daughter. A teenage daughter. What did he know about teenagers? Absolutely nothing, that's what. The last thing he needed was to fall for the pretty face belonging to a hurricane of a woman that threatened to disrupt his entire life. So... he wouldn't. He'd help her when she needed it and then keep on keeping on. That's what he did. He was good at it. He was content that way. So why did he seem so *off* tonight? Why did he want to walk back over to the raggedy old cabin and help Reesa unpack her house and get to know her?

Safety. That was it. It must be it. Some random woman sweet talks his grandmother into letting her live in the old family summer cabin and he was bound to be protective. She could be psycho for all they knew. It was his duty to uncover who she was and why she was here. From the sounds of it, she moved around a lot. Didn't even seem bothered by the fact she uprooted her daughter over and over again in the process. There was a story there. A why to the reason she lived in such a way. And he was going to find out.

CHAPTER THREE

Clare shuffled down the hallway towards the kitchen, the smell of burnt bacon and toast surprising her less than the organized rooms before her. Trooper hurried into the room ahead of her and took a small leap to land on the freshly fitted couch cover and burrow down into the comfy cushions. "Mom?"

Reesa's head popped out of the small pantry. "Morning, sunshine!"

"What happened in here?" Clare continued to circle and stare at their new little house. It almost looked homey. Almost.

"I unpacked a bit."

"A bit," Clare agreed, impressed.

"Just don't look in my bedroom. This is as far as I got. I put any of your boxes along the hallway there." She pointed to a row of boxes neatly stacked.

"And breakfast?"

"Right, well, I tried." She pointed to a plate with the overly crispy bacon and blackened bread. "I'll try to get to the store in the next few days to get some toaster pastries or something. Billy Lou bought actual food." Reesa looked flabbergasted. "Like food-food, as in I have to actually cook it by standing at the stove."

"You're a woman of many talents."

Reesa laughed. "Why thank you." She took a bow. "I'm organizing all the other groceries. She really did hook us up." She shook a package of chocolate sandwich cookies. "Gotta love her for these."

"There's also ice cream. I put it in the freezer last night. If it hasn't melted."

Reesa's brow furrowed.

"Have you seen how old that fridge is?"

"I like it. It's vintage."

"Yes, but it's tiny. We won't be able to have much in there."

"Do we ever anyway?"

"True." Clare took a bite of a piece of bacon and gave a little shrug of acceptance as she took another bite. "What time did Theo leave?"

"An hour or so after he brought the blankets. He helped me unload the rest of the trailer. Did you sleep okay?"

"Like a baby. That heavy blue quilt is awesome. I hate to give it back."

"I know, right? The blanket I used felt like a dream and smelled like one too."

Clare's brows lifted in amusement. "Oh really?"

"Yeah, did yours not smell?"

"They smelled like someone else's house."

"But they weren't all masculine smelling?"

"Sort of, but I guess I didn't think about it."

"Oh." Reesa ducked back into the pantry.

"But clearly you did." Clare laughed. "Mom? There something you not telling me? You have a crush on the lumberjack?"

"Ha! Lumberjack—that's funny. But don't be absurd." Reesa stepped out and shook her head as she surveyed which task to tackle next.

"You sure?"

"Yes."

"So, if he pulled up to the cabin this morning and you were wearing... that." Clare pointed to Reesa's skimpy pajama shorts and tattered ACDC sleep shirt. "You'd be completely okay with him seeing you like that?"

"Yes. Why would I care? This is my house now. I can look how I want. And I'm not trying to impress some overly bearded gladiator."

"Well, that's good to know, because he just pulled up." Clare pointed out the front window as Reesa's eyes darted out the glass.

"Shoot!" Reesa ran to her room and caught her little toe on the door jam, yelping in pain as a knock on the door sounded.

"Don't worry. I got it," Clare called on a laugh. "Morning," she greeted, waving Theo inside.

She saw his gaze survey the room and a spark of appreciation of her mom's hard work briefly appeared. "Mom's changing."

"I brought these." He handed a box of donuts to Clare and her face lit into a luminous smile. "Suit him up, Mom!" she yelled. "For we officially have a knight in shining armor!"

Reesa limped up the hall dressed in denim shorts and a fitted tee showcasing The Beatles walking along Abbey Road. "Are those donuts?" Her eyes gleamed.

"They are." Clare fanned the box beneath her mother's nose and both women stared at him with stars in their eyes.

"Yep. Our knight," Reesa confirmed.

Trooper perked up on the couch as Theo stepped inside and happily barked before lunging off the sofa and running to Theo's feet. He flopped over for a belly rub, which Theo gladly gave him. "He sleep alright?"

"Like a baby." Clare brushed an affectionate hand over the dog's head. "He kept me warm too."

"I checked in on them about one this morning and they were snuggled up and both snoring."

"I don't snore," Clare objected and a light flush staining her cheeks at her mother mentioning it.

"*He* does." Theo pointed to Trooper before tapping the dog's nose. "I'm headed into town. You need anything?" He looked at her list on the fridge and other than the word: Beer, nothing was listed. "Easy enough."

"It's not a real need. I just hit a wall about midnight and thought it sure sounded good at the time. I opted for another cup of coffee instead and then knocked out two more hours of unpacking. So I guess the coffee was the productive choice." Reesa beamed proudly.

"You don't look like you barely slept," Theo commented, his subtle compliment not going unnoticed by Clare.

Reesa laughed. "Well, thanks, but I feel like it. My limbs are having a hard time keeping up with my ambition. Thanks for the blankets, by the way. I still haven't unboxed bedding, so they came in handy last night. Just out of curiosity, what soap do you use?"

Surprise had his brows slightly lifting and Clare snorted behind her donut before taking a bite.

"Soap?"

"Yeah," Reesa mimicked taking a shower. "Soap." "Uh…"

"She liked the smell of your blankets," Clare mouthed around the donut in her cheek and rolled her eyes.

"Oh."

"Yeah, I was surprised too." Reesa pointed to his face. "But they smelled amazing."

"Umm…. Thanks… I think." Theo rubbed a hand over his beard, suddenly self-conscious.

"Anyways," Reesa waved him further inside. "Coffee? I have a fresh pot." She walked over and began pouring three mugs, handing one to her daughter. "She's a monster and drinks it black. One of many bad habits I've blessed her with. You?"

Clare patted the table for him to come and sit. "Cream, if you have it."

"I do. Your grandmother saw to that. Vanilla, okay? That's what she bought."

"That's fine." He watched as she heavily poured cream into the cup and then walked it over. She sat in the other free chair and grabbed a donut. "I thought I'd take your trailer with me and drop it off at the rental yard."

Reesa paused in her bite at his generosity. "Really? It's Sunday. Are they open?"

"No, but I know Tim and will let him know."

"Oh. Well, yeah, that'd be great. Thanks."

"And I'll be back later to help my grandmother move the Corvette back to her place."

"We could do that this morning," Reesa offered. "I could drive it over there and you could bring me back here on your way to town?"

"You just want to drive it again," Clare outed her.

"Duh." Reesa smiled. "But it would also remove it from my sight, and I will no longer be tempted by its irresistible charm. I'm a sucker for a pretty face."

"Then I guess we could take care of that here soon. As long as you don't go crazy and take off down the road in it." Theo looked to Clare to gauge that possibility and the teen giggled.

"I'm not Vin Diesel," Reesa assured him. "I won't drive it off a cliff and parachute myself into your grandmother's yard."

"What?" Theo asked in confusion.

"Do you even watch movies?" Reesa asked. "Vin Diesel, XXX... You know, the whole I'm angry at the senator, so I'm going to steal his car and drive it off a cliff and film it for him."

"Yeah, never seen that one," Theo admitted.

"Don't worry. No one has," Clare assured him. "It was a bust, but my mom loves it."

"I wouldn't say I love it. I liked it. I like Vin Diesel. I just want to hug him when I see him on screen."

"Hug him?" Theo took a sip of his coffee, his eyes watching her closely.

"Yes. Hug. As in wrap my arms around him and have those big muscley arms give me a squeeze. I think it would feel nice." She set her cup down and then slapped a hand to the table making the other two jump. "Okay, so I'll grab my shoes. I'm ready." She left the room and Theo looked to Clare.

Without asking, she answered his unspoken question. "Yes, she is always like this. You learn to love it." Grinning, she helped herself to another donut. "Thanks again for Trooper last night. It's always a bit weird the first night in a new place.

And this place is so quiet it was... unnerving. It was nice to have him with me when I got nervous."

"No problem. You need him tonight?"

"No, that's okay. I think he missed you." She blushed at admitting that to him as if she were also disappointed the dog was ready to go home. "I'll just leave my radio on tonight for some background noise."

"You lived in the city before moving here?"

"Not really the city, but in town. We had a great house on the corner of Old Main. An old colonial place. Mom fixed it up and we were able to sell it for twice what we paid for it. But it was my favorite house we've lived in so far."

"And how many houses have you lived in?"

Clare looked heavenward and mentally tallied. "Eight... no, nine... wait... if we count the barn, I'd guess it'd be ten."

"Barn?" His tone held the slight inflection of disappointment, but their conversation was cut short by Reesa entering the room slipping a shoe on her foot.

"Ready?"

His eyes lingered on her exposed legs a moment before he stood and walked his cup to the sink. "Sure."

"You alright staying here by yourself? Or do you want to go?" Reesa asked.

"I'll be fine. I'm going to work on unpacking my closet. Find my sheets and stuff."

"Alright, looks like it is just you and me, Paul Walker."

"Who?" Theo asked.

"Honestly," Reesa threw up her hands. "Where's your pop culture knowledge, Theo? You're killing me." She led the way out the door explaining the Vin Diesel and Paul Walker partnership in all the Fast and the Furious movies, all her words falling on deaf ears as Theo still had no clue as to what she was talking about. "And you're a mechanic... you should be all about car movies, right?"

"Maybe I don't want to watch movies about cars since I'm around them all day."

"But you have the best opportunities to drop movie quotes all day long working around cars."

"Why would I do that?"

"Because it's fun." Reesa paused at the door of the Corvette. "Well, this is it, baby. Our relationship has come to an end. It was short, but thrilling." She rubbed a hand over the top of the door as she opened it. "It's not you, it's me. Actually, it's me and him." She thumbed over her shoulder towards Theo. "We just aren't comfortable with this arrangement. And though it feels right between us, we both know it's wrong."

"You done?" Theo asked, unamused at her playful banter and snapping her back into seriousness.

"I guess." She sighed as she slid behind the wheel. "Following you."

He nodded and shut her door.

~

Billy Lou stood on her massive front porch, the white railing wrapping all the way around the ranch-style home. Her perfectly styled white hair was combed into an elegant French twist and fastened off with a silver swirled clip. She'd always been beautiful, Theo thought. No matter her age, his grandmother stood with grace, dignity, and style. The house matched her perfectly. The pristine flower beds and landscaping, the lush shade trees, and the overhanging of wisteria that draped along the edges of her front porch created a picturesque, magazine-worthy photo. The scowl on her face, on the other hand, did not match the happy exterior she presented. "I hate you're not going to use that thing." She hugged Reesa and her face slipped into its usual smile.

"I just can't." Reesa squeezed her hands. "Trust me, it's eating me up that I can't."

"I know, honey." Billy Lou nodded towards her grandson as he made his way to the porch, picking up a stray tree limb along his way. "How'd you manage to nudge him out of bed this morning?"

"I didn't. He's the one that showed up at my house. Bearing gifts too. I think Clare has elevated him to hero status for bringing her donuts."

Billy Lou's eyes gleamed as she turned her attention and newfound interest towards Theo. "Theodore."

He leaned down and kissed her cheek. "Mornin', Grandma."

"You two come on in and have some coffee. You like French pressed, Reesa?"

"I like any coffee, Billy Lou."

"That-a girl. Come on now." She waved them inside as she walked towards a luxurious kitchen with sweeping oak cabinets and polished granite countertops.

"We can't stay long, Grandma. I've got to get Reesa back to the cabin and I'm taking her trailer to Tim this morning."

"Oh, posh, Theodore, Tim can wait. Besides, I am just hungry for company this mornin'. I was tempted to come by the cabin, but I didn't want you to think I was checking up on you so soon."

"You're welcome anytime," Reesa invited.

"It seems someone else beat me to it this morning though." Billy Lou nodded towards Theo.

"Theo's gone above and beyond," Reesa explained. "He helped me unload the rest of the trailer, loaned us some blankets for the beds last night, and even brought donuts this morning. I don't know what I'll do once we settle in and he grows annoyed with us."

Billy Lou laughed. "Oh honey, Theo's annoyed by everybody. Don't take it personal."

"Thanks, Grandma." Theo's dry tone had the women grinning.

"Now, tell me, Reesa, what is it you do for work?"

"I crochet."

"Crochet? As in knit?" Theo asked curiously.

"No. As in, I crochet. It's different than knitting."

"And you make stuff and sell it?"

She laughed. "Something like that. I create patterns, sell them online, and then film educational how-to videos for certain stitches and techniques. I market mostly online and it's flexible. Plus, I'm able to work from anywhere, which is nice."

"That is wonderful." Billy Lou took a long sip of her coffee and eyed Theo over the top of it to signal him to ask the next question.

"That why you're free to move so much?"

"Pretty much. We aren't anchored anywhere due to a job, so we can float wherever the wind blows us."

"An adventurous lifestyle." Smiling, Billy Lou toasted towards her. "I'm not cut out for it. I've lived in this house for over fifty years and have no desire to leave it."

"I don't blame you. It's beautiful. It's like a little slice of heaven."

"I think so. Jerry and I worked hard to make it so. Jerry is my late husband."

"The owner of the magnificent red beast out there?"

"Yes. Though that was a complete waste of money and time, in my opinion. It was the one purchase we did not agree on." Billy Lou pointed to Theo. "I've tried to get Theo to take it off my hands, but he refuses."

"Dad would kill me for it."

"Your daddy would have to go through me first. And his fingers will never touch it." Billy Lou's sharp tone surprised Reesa, but she didn't comment, for which Theo was grateful. She didn't need to know about the dysfunctional side of his family. "So, Reesa, you have family tucked away somewhere?"

"Here and there, but the relationship is estranged."

"I'm sorry to hear that. It's hard when that happens."

"It was at first, but Clare and I have made it work. She's my world, and I'll do whatever I have to in order to protect her from what I experienced." Theo zoned in on her face as she spoke, the smidgen of hurt and anger slipping through before she realized her mood had darkened and quickly changed course. "Clare's great though. I couldn't have asked for a better kid."

"A lot of that has to do with parenting," Billy Lou complimented. "I see the special bond you two share. I think it's wonderful. And I hope to get to know the two of you better."

"Likewise." Reesa set her empty cup on the shining countertop. "That was exquisite coffee, Billy Lou. Thank you."

"Oh, anytime, sweetie. We should make this a regular thing. Sunday mornin' coffee. I'd love it."

"Me too." Reesa looked to Theo. "Ready? I don't want to hold up your day. And I want to be able to help Clare with her closet. Tomorrow is her first day at school and I know it will take hours to pick the perfect outfit."

"Bless her heart." Billy Lou held a hand to her heart. "Oh, I arranged her a ride tomorrow. There's this sweet boy named Teddy who lives up the street. He's a safe driver, been driving since he was ten around these parts. He's sixteen, but responsible."

"Grandma, Reesa may not feel comfortable with—"

"I know, that's why I told him I would let him know. I was going to talk to Reesa first."

"I hate to not take her myself on her first day." Reesa looked nervous at the idea of Clare facing a new place without their usual routine.

"I can pick you both up and take you," Theo offered. "And then if we let Teddy know to introduce himself to Clare tomorrow, she can let you know if she'd mind riding with him."

"I... this is a lot. You've already done so much for us. I hate to ask you to swing by the house so early."

"I don't mind." Theo shrugged his shoulders. "I have to be at my garage by eight, so it's on the way."

"Not if you have to bring me back to the house afterwards."

"I figured we'd look over your car in the morning."

"Oh, right. Well, I guess that would work." Reesa nodded. "Thank you, again. I'm continually amazed at the kindness of complete strangers. Especially ones who look like—"

"Is this another beard joke?" Theo interrupted. "Can we just stop with the beard jokes?"

Reesa and Billy Lou laughed, and he rolled his eyes. "I'm leaving. If you're wanting a ride home instead of a three-mile hike through the woods, you better come on."

"I think he's starting to know me," Reesa whispered on a giggle to Billy Lou. She hugged the older woman one last time.

"You dish it out, honey. He needs it. See you later." She waved them off and Theo slowly made his way back to the cabin.

"Your grandmother is one classy gal. I like her."

"She's pretty special."

"I never really knew my grandparents. They died when I was young. Both sets."

"What about your parents?"

"We're estranged."

"Ah, so that's who you were talking about."

"Yep." Her clipped answer left him curious.

"Where do they live?"

"Hot Springs."

He tapped the breaks in surprise, and she gasped at the slight lunge amidst their momentum. "Hot Springs?"

"Yes."

"Do they know you're living in Piney?"

"No. Not yet."

"Wh-how-why-what?"

She snickered at his confusion. "Yeah, same. I don't know why I moved so close either. I had this momentary lapse in judgment, I guess. With Clare about to finish her sophomore year of high school, I just started thinking about how they might want to see her, meet her, and see that she's this wonderful human being. But then we moved, and I've sort of been inwardly panicking about them meeting, so I haven't made it happen yet."

"Wait, your parents have never met your daughter?" Shocked, he pulled up to the cabin and parked, Clare and Trooper playing fetch outside. The happy teenager waving before taking the slobbery tennis ball and throwing it again.

"No, they haven't." Reesa's voice grew sad. "I'm terrible, aren't I?"

"I didn't say that."

"But you're thinking it."

"No, actually, I'm not. I don't know your story," Theo replied. "I'm sure you have your reasons for the way you've lived your life. It's not my place to judge. Besides, my parents aren't exactly all rainbows and sunshine either. My relationship with my dad is tense, at best. And my mother, when she decides to lay off the martinis before noon, can be sweet, but an air of disappointment lingers when we're in the same room."

"Ah, so you disappointed them."

"You could say that."

"Did you get knocked up at sixteen and refuse to give the baby up? Because that's my story."

He looked at her then, his eyes studying her. Her own dark gaze took on a slight sheen that said she was preparing herself for his rejection too. "Sixteen?"

"Yep. Tada! Unwed teen mother." She raised her hand. "My parents dropped me off at a pregnancy support center and I haven't seen them since."

"Sixteen years ago?"

"Well, fifteen... about to be sixteen years ago. But yes."

"I'm sorry."

She shrugged. "It's life. It happens. It moves along and we make the best of it, right?"

"Couldn't have been easy."

"It wasn't, but it's gotten easier over the years. And look what I got out of the deal." She pointed to Clare as she laid on her back and Trooper attacked her with kisses. "She's the best thing to ever happen to me. I'd say I came out on top in the deal."

Theo harumphed in agreement. "Yeah. Not bad."

Reesa opened her door, Trooper perking up at the sound. When Theo stepped out of his truck, Trooper sprinted over and then back to Clare with excited yips for her to throw the ball again. "About time. I thought you were leaving me to unpack all the yarn." Clare motioned towards the house.

"Billy Lou wanted to visit," Reesa explained.

"I figured. Hey, I followed the directions on the back of one of those freezer meals Billy Lou bought. It's in the slow cooker."

"We have a slow cooker?" Reesa asked.

"Apparently." Clare looked as surprised as her mother. "It's some sort of Italian chicken pasta."

"Thank you, Billy Lou!" Reesa fist pumped into the air in celebration. "Want to eat lunch with us later?" she asked, taking Theo and Clare by surprise.

Noticing her daughter's intrigued expression had him shaking his head. "I would, but I need to tackle some work in my garden today."

"You have a garden?" Reesa asked with amusement. "People really do that sort of thing?"

"Mom." Clare slapped a palm to her face in embarrassment and Theo chuckled.

"People really do. Or so I've heard."

"Wow." Reesa grinned. "Well, have fun with that. Thanks for the ride and taking the trailer with you. And for tomorrow morning." She drum-rolled her hands on his arm in a friendly pat.

"You just made it awkward," Clare warned and then laughed as Theo nodded.

Reesa nudged him towards his truck. "You'll get used to me. See you tomorrow."

He whistled over his shoulder and Trooper hurried after him, jumping into the cab of the truck one step ahead of Theo. He watched as Reesa affectionately rubbed a hand over Clare's long ponytail on their way back into the cabin before tossing him one last wave. From what he could tell, Reesa was a great mother, and though odd, a good person. Time would tell. In the meantime, he backed his truck towards the trailer and set to work.

CHAPTER FOUR

"Okay, now if you get nervous, just avoid eye contact." Reesa pointed her hand towards the windshield as Theo turned into the local school's drive.

"I'll be fine, Mom." Clare shook her head. "I've been to a bazillion schools. I've got my own coping mechanisms, thanks."

"Well, just look for that Teddy guy Billy Lou told me about. She said he'd find you."

Theo pointed his finger toward one of the front pillars to a tall, fit boy with clean-cut hair casually holding a backpack on his shoulder. "What?" Reesa shook her head. "No, no, no, no, no. Absolutely not."

"What? What's wrong?" Theo asked.

"Are you kidding me right now?" Reesa looked at him in frustration. "He's a dreamboat. You can't introduce my daughter to a dreamboat on her first day!"

Clare laughed from the backseat. "Mom, chill. He looks nice."

"Um, yeah... that's how they get you."

"Theo, help me out here or she's going to hold me hostage in the truck," Clare begged.

"He's a good kid. Plus, I'll give him the nod," Theo encouraged.

"What *nod*?" Reesa asked.

"*The* nod." Theo imitated an intimidating head tilt and narrowed eyes. "He'll know what it means."

"Great. Now I have a surly bodyguard *and* a crazy mom. Awesome." Clare climbed out of the truck when they reached the curb and Teddy walked forward. He bent down to peer into the passenger side window as Reesa rolled it down.

"Mr. Whitley," Teddy greeted. He extended his hand to Reesa. "Ms. Tate. I'm Teddy Graham. Yes, that's legit my name." He flushed at the absurdity.

"Nice to meet you. Clare—" She pointed to her daughter on the curb.

"I'll show her around."

"Clare, you good? I could come in." Reesa started to unbuckle her seat belt and Clare hurried forward. "No, no. I'm good, Mom. I'll just follow Teddy. Thanks for the ride, Theo." She waved, giving Reesa a small smile of assurance.

"Okay. Have a good day. I love you. Don't do drugs!" Reesa called after them. "Watch those hands, Teddy Graham!" she yelled after them, the boy turning back towards the truck to assure his innocence, but Clare forced him to continue walking towards the school.

"Ugh, he's adorable." Reesa rolled up the window. "Why did he have to be adorable?"

Theo smirked. "He's a good kid. You've got nothing to worry about."

"Right. Well, I'm going to be a nervous wreck all day. That's how I get when she starts a new school. And it's certainly how I feel when she's spending time with a cute boy... all chummy."

"How about we focus on your car this morning? That will take your mind off Clare."

"I doubt it, but I will try."

"Well, I can give you the information now and take you home, or I can still take you to the garage and show you. What's your choice?"

"Show me the damage."

"Okay." He turned down a side street and pulled in front of his mechanic shop, two other vehicles already there.

Reesa followed him inside and watched in silence as he went through his morning routine of checking a clipboard slung over his messy desk before booting up the computer. He walked towards a back room and grabbed a light blue button up shirt and began snapping it over his white t-shirt. His name tag stated: T.J., and the garage's insignia was stitched across the breast pocket. "Follow me." He motioned towards a door leading into the open bays where one man was halfway on his back tucked under a small sedan and the other was shoulders deep in the hood of a pickup. He walked her towards her car and her heart sank.

"Internally, your car is fine," Theo reported. "In fact, if you wanted, you could drive it home as is. If you're wanting the body repaired, it will be a few days. Luckily for you, the main body frame isn't bent so we'd just be replacing the door. I found one available and can have it here in a couple of days."

"It's an easy fix?"

"Yep."

"And how much is it?"

"Depends. Did you call your insurance company?"

"No. We never exchanged insurance."

"Ah. True. Well, it's up to you. I'm covering the cost either way because it was my fault, so it's your choice if you want to claim it."

"Just fix it. I don't know if I really have it in me right now to deal with insurance phone calls and the back and forth."

"Alright. I'll get the door ordered today then." He tapped a pencil against his palm as the man under the sedan slid out. He hopped to his feet and flashed a charming smile at Reesa. "Mornin', ma'am."

"Morning."

"Mike, this is Reesa Tate. She's new in town," Theo introduced.

"Aahhhh, the new pretty lady livin' up at that cabin of yours. Yeah, Betty Hoke mentioned it the other day over at Seymore's. Nice to meet you." Mike extended his hand and Reesa gave it a hearty shake.

"Likewise." The man's eyes lingered a moment on her face, then he offered a sly wink before walking back to his work. He was somewhat good looking, Reesa thought. A bit rough around the edges, which wasn't really her type, but he seemed friendly enough. As she walked behind Theo back towards the office area, she felt Mike's eyes on her, though, and they didn't sit well. She was familiar with that feeling. A woman could always tell when a man's gaze was that of a potential friend or date versus a creeper. And at the moment, a tingle of trepidation fluttered up and down her spine telling her to tread carefully around Mike. Warning bells rang in her head, but not the good kind. There was no Hallelujah Chorus playing up there, instead, the Jaws theme song seemed to flood her thoughts.

"Reesa?" Theo asked, his deep brown eyes studying her with concern.

She jumped, not realizing she'd zoned out thinking about giant sharks and open water. "Hm? What?"

"You alright?"

"Oh." She flushed. "Yeah. Sorry. Spaced out a minute. What were you saying?"

"I said I ordered the door. Want me to take you home?"

"I can walk."

"It's ten miles out of town."

"Right." She felt her cheeks flood pink again and she nervously stepped closer to him when Mike walked into the office to fetch a bottle of water from the mini fridge. Mike's eyes locked on hers as she tucked herself as close to Theo as possible. Her elbow brushed against him, and she accidentally stepped on his work boot in the process, but she attempted to stay calm and collected. Mike smiled and gave a quick nod before heading back into the garage. Her shoulders relaxed until Theo cleared his throat and pointed to her foot on top of his. "Right," she said again, quickly shifting away from him.

"You sure you're okay? Did Mike say something to you?"

"No." She waved her hands to ward off the topic. "No. I'm fine. Just jumpy this morning. Must be getting used to Clare being gone again or something. Um... if you don't mind, could I just walk through town for a while and explore? Maybe I could meet you back over here at eleven and then you take me home?"

"That's fine."

"Great." She forced a smile. "Thanks, Theo... for the door." She pointed at his computer as she backed her way out of his office and hurried towards the sidewalk along the street. What was wrong with her? Mike was just a small-town mechanic with an overabundance of confidence. He wasn't a threat to her. But her body begged to differ. She still felt the crash of adrenaline from that fight or flight encounter. She would make sure to tell Clare to steer clear of Mike. She popped her head up at the sound of light jazz music spilling from a tiny coffee shop tucked amongst the old buildings of downtown. Nestled between a resale shop and pizza joint, Java Jamie beckoned her with the tantalizing smell of roasting coffee beans. She walked inside and immediately felt her body relax.

"Be with you in a minute!" a voice called from the back kitchen.

Reesa studied the menu, the inventive and creative drinks sounding better with each line she read. A woman, roughly her age, with carrot orange curls over a round, rosy-cheeked face stepped from the back room carrying a tray of luscious croissants covered in flecks of chocolate. "Mornin'," she greeted warmly. "Just let me put these in the cabinet here," she grunted as she bent over to slide the tray in the glass display case amongst other baked delicacies and then lifted her friendly blue eyes to Reesa. "Hi. Welcome to Java Jamie. I'm Jamie." She waved her hands over herself and gave a small giggle. "Guess you probably already knew that. What can I get ya?"

"I'm typically a black coffee kind of girl, but I will admit the Riddler's Latte sounds intriguing. What is that?"

"Ah." Jamie pointed to the sign in front of her register. "It changes daily. If you guess the riddle, you get a latte of your choice for free." Her eyes danced. "I like games."

"I have cities, but no houses. I have mountains, but no trees. I have water, but no fish. What am I?" Reesa read. She tapped her chin a second. "Cities, mountains, and water... a picture of some sort."

Jamie's smile widened in excitement, and she anxiously clapped her hands, her short, plump body giving two excited little jumps. "You're so close."

Reesa read the clue one more time and then snapped. "A map!"

"Ding ding ding!" Jamie reached over to the bell on her counter and hit it five times and hooted in celebration. "We have a winner! Wow, first try. Normally people give up and just order something different."

"People are no fun," Reesa replied and had the barista chuckling.

"That is the truth. So, what kind of latte do you want?"

"Surprise me."

"Oooooh." Jamie rubbed her hands together. "Great mind, daring request... I can tell we're going to be friends. What's your name?"

"Reesa Tate."

"Oh! The woman who lives over in Billy Lou's cabin?"

"Let me guess, Betty Hoke told you?" Reesa asked, following Mike's earlier response.

"No, Billy Lou. She's excited to have you. You have a daughter, right?"

"Yes. Clare. She started school today."

"Oh man, that's hard. First day at a new school."

"She's a champ, and Billy Lou had a boy named Teddy lined up to show her around."

"Teddy Graham?" Jamie asked.

"Yes."

"Love that boy." Jamie smiled. "Could just serve him right up with my honey butter biscuits." She spotted Reesa's frown and then sobered. "Was it something I said?"

"No. Apparently, I'm just at that stage in motherhood where the thought of a cute, nice boy being near my daughter bothers me. It's new."

Jamie giggled, her jolly demeanor infectious, and Reesa relaxed.

"How much trouble do you think a boy named after a cookie could be?" Jamie asked, holding up a finger to put a pause on their conversation as her phone rang. She answered in a joyful tone: "Java Jamie, where the coffee is hot and so am I!"

Reesa beamed at the woman's positive energy and began slowly walking around and looking at all the photos and paintings throughout the shop.

"I'll get them whipped up for you, T.J." She penciled down a note. "You sending Mike to fetch'em?" She adjusted the phone on her shoulder. "Oh really? The big man himself is going to grace me with his presence? Give me five minutes, I need to fix my hair and put on my face," she teased, her voice hitching into a snorted laugh as she hung up the phone. She swiped a tear from her eye as she shook her head in amusement. "Oh!" She snapped her fingers. "Let me get you that latte." She rushed around her little nook and set to work bringing forth bewitching smells. "So, what brings you to Piney?" Jamie asked.

"Life," Reesa replied and shrugged. "Just wanted a new place."
"Billy Lou said you're like some big online sensation with crafts."

Reesa smiled affectionately. "She would say that."

"Gotta love that woman," Jamie continued. "She's like— dream goals for when I get old. I want to look like her, dress like her, act like her..."

"I totally know what you mean," Reesa agreed.

"Billy Lou takes crap from no one," Jamie explained. "She's the best of Piney and everyone knows it." The door opened and Jamie looked up with a friendly wave. "I'm getting them ready," she called.

Reesa turned to find Theo standing behind her.

"Should have known you'd find the coffee shop." He stepped forward and Reesa's day grew brighter. She liked being around Theo. So far, he was her only friend, and just that small comfort had her stepping towards him.

"Couldn't get enough of me, hm?" she asked, as she elbowed him in the side.

Jamie watched their interaction as her hands moved in fast motion, preparing the order he'd called in.

"Or maybe I just need coffee because someone had me up earlier than normal for the school drop-off line."

"You volunteered." She pointed an accusatory finger up at him and she saw a slight glimmer in his eyes that told her he was teasing.

"What will it be Jamie?" He opened his wallet and she rattled off his total. He slipped out several bills and dropped what change she gave him into the tip jar. "Keep her out of trouble." He tilted his head towards Reesa.

"Uh oh." Jamie snickered. "You already have the neighborhood watch after you."

Reesa rolled her eyes and watched Theo's hands. Big hands, she realized, long fingers, neat nails, and— She interrupted her own thoughts with a mental scolding. "Stop it."

"What?" he asked.

She flushed, realizing her inward thought had come out of her mouth. "Oh, nothing. I was just... mentally shaving your face and realized it was no use."

He narrowed his eyes as Jamie laughed. "See T.J., I'm not the only one who thinks that beard needs to go. It's been years since we've seen that handsome face of yours." Jamie held up a hand to block her mouth from Theo's view, her eyes sparkling as she did not mask the register of her voice, "And handsome it is."

"I'm leaving," Theo growled, grabbing the carry tray of the three coffees he planned to take back to his garage.

"Don't be embarrassed, T. You know I love you." Jamie waved at his retreating back and Reesa held up a finger to signal that she'd return but needed to chase him down.

"Theo, wait a minute." She rushed after him as he stepped outside onto the sidewalk, his tall frame towering over her as she looked up at him.

"What is it?" he tucked his free hand into the front pocket of his jeans, the other holding the drink tray. He already had a grease stain on his shirt, and a worn bandana hanging from his back pocket.

She slipped her arms around his waist and rested her head against his broad chest in a tight hug. She felt him squirm and then pulled back. "Have a good morning." She hurried back inside to find a stunned Jamie standing with her mouth open at what she just witnessed. Reesa turned to see Theo still standing on the sidewalk as if he didn't know what to do.

"Did I just—"

"Uh huh." Jamie nodded.
"Out there?" Reesa asked.

"Right in the open." Jamie grinned.

"Why?"

"I'm dying to know." Jamie began her jittery bouncing again as she squealed. "T.J. Whitley's stunned out there. You electric eel, you." She pointed chummily at Reesa. "Look at 'im! Look at 'im!" She pointed over Reesa's shoulder as Theo glanced around to make sure no one witnessed the embrace before taking a tense step in the direction of his garage. Jamie guffawed. "Love *it!*"

Reesa slapped a palm over her face. "I'm continually making him feel awkward and all he's done is be nice to me. It was gratitude. A gratitudal hug. Gratitudal? Grat-i-tudal... Is that a word?"

"I don't think so." Jamie continued smiling as she slid Reesa her latte. "It's a mocha with a twist." She mimicked the fifties dance move as she watched Reesa take the first sip.

"Mmm." Reesa's brows lifted in delighted surprise. "Is that butterscotch?"

"Sure is." Jamie beamed.

"Well, it's delicious, and I love your shop. I will probably come here every day."

"That's what I like to hear."

"I might even be able to crochet here too. Get out of the house every now and then."

"So that's what you do? Crochet?"

"Yes." Reesa smiled. "Normally I'm sporting something I've made, but I haven't unpacked my closet yet."

Jamie waved away the oversight. "Closets are the worst."

"And then there's the boxes and boxes of yarn. Though I will admit, I actually like organizing that."

"Well, come on in anytime. It's nice to meet a new face and a new friend."

Warmed by Jamie's upbeat personality and genuine kindness, Reesa toasted her latte towards the cheery red head. "Same. See ya around, hot thang."

"Ooooooh." Reesa walked out on a laugh as she saw Jamie's reflection dancing behind her counter.

~

Theo waited in the car pickup line and slowly pulled forward as Clare and Teddy walked up to his passenger side. Though they hadn't mapped out a plan for after school, he figured the girl would need a ride since he'd dropped Reesa off at the cabin before lunch and hadn't heard a word from her since. Clare's smile faltered a bit when she didn't see her mom riding shot gun, but Teddy opened the door for her ,and she slid inside. "I'll see you tomorrow, Clare."

"Thanks, Teddy." She waved as she began buckling her seat belt and Theo tossed a half wave over the steering wheel to the boy and pulled forward in line to leave. "Thanks for coming to pick me up."

"No problem." His hands were covered in dried grease and grime, and his truck held the light scent of sweat on top of it, but he didn't have time to worry about that. He had to get back to the shop as soon as he dropped Clare off.

"I'm surprised Mom didn't come too."

"Well... I was already in town."

"She forgot me, didn't she?" Clare asked. She noticed his grip tighten on the steering wheel and sighed. "Hopefully that means she's been busy unpacking. Thanks for coming. Tomorrow I will ride with Teddy. He's a cool guy."

Silence hung in the truck and Theo cleared his throat. "So, what did you think about the school?"

"Not too bad. I walked by the trophy case and saw your picture." She bit back a smile as he rubbed a hand over his face. "Actually, Teddy showed it to me. He sort of worships you, by the way."

"He shouldn't."

"You still have hero status when it comes to baseball. Did you know they have your picture in the boy's locker room?"

Horrified, Theo turned to her. "What?"

She laughed. "That's what he said. Right next to a poster of some basketball player. I don't remember his name though."

"Justin Monroe?" Theo asked.

"That's it! How'd you know?"

"Star player for Lake Hamilton High, class of 2007."

"Ah. I see. You mean they don't have any newer posters since you guys? Wow... the teams must suck."

Theo's deep chuckle had her smile broadening.

"What's your story, Theo?" Clare turned in her seat to face him better. "You grew up here. You have an awesome grandmother. You aren't married, or at least from what I can tell you aren't." She pointed at his ring finger. "So, tell me."

"Tell you what?"

"About *you*," she restated with annoyance at him for procrastinating.

"You about summed it up."

"Come on, there's more to you than that. You're super nice, have a great dog, and a garden, from what you said this weekend. What else?"

Uncomfortable with the interrogation, he shrugged. "There's not much to tell. You've hit my high points."

Rolling her eyes, Clare defiantly crossed her arms over her chest and tilted her chin up just enough that she looked like her mother. "You're being difficult on purpose."

"Add that to my list of traits."

"You dating anyone?"

He narrowed his eyes at her before turning back to the road.

"Clearly that's a no," she confirmed. "Do you have any siblings?"

"Two."

"See, we're getting somewhere." Clare motioned like she was pulling invisible rope between them. "Do they live in Piney?"

"No."

She waved for him to elaborate.

On an exhausted sigh, he acquiesced. "My older brother is an attorney in Hot Springs. He's married and has two kids. My younger sister lives in Louisiana. She's working on her master's degree in biology at Louisiana State University. She's not married, nor does she have kids. There. That work?"

"Cool." Clare grinned, looking pleased with herself. She rolled her hand for him to carry on.

"Oh, right... what about you Clare? You married? Have kids?" His exaggerated and forced upbeat tone had her snorting before she laughed and tossed a quarter from his cupholder at him.

"No. But I have a crazy, amazing mom who happens to also be my best friend. I love bubble gum, but rarely get to chew it. And I make a mean omelet."

His lips quirked. "Why do you not get to chew bubble gum?"

"Mom thinks it just adds extra mileage to your jaw bones. She said we should use all we can for talking, not chewing gum."

"That explains a lot," Theo agreed, moving his hand like an open and closing mouth.

"Yeah, she likes to talk. She also says that when a woman chews gum people assume her IQ is lower than it really is."

That comment surprised him, but he knew it stemmed from someone treating Reesa badly or making that comment to her and it hit. He wondered how old she was when someone said that to her. The thought angered him. "Gum is gum. What's your favorite kind?"

"I like green Double Bubble. You always see the pink and blue packaged Double Bubble, but the green and purple are harder to find. But the green is my favorite. My mom used to put some in my stocking every year at Christmas in a little plastic sandwich bag. She'd tell me Santa must have liked it too, and he gave me his personal stash. It took me years to figure out she just couldn't afford fancy packaging and that she'd buy it by the piece at the local gas station when she saw it. It would take her months to collect all the green ones." Clare's voice softly trailed off.

"That's a great story."

"She's always made sure I've had it all."

"You don't seem spoiled to me."

Clare grinned. "I have my moments. But I'm about to be sixteen, so I'm allowed to have dramatic flare-ups every now and then. I just try not to let it get too out of hand. Mom's worked hard for what we have. She's taught me so much when it comes to life and business. She's built her business from the ground up, on her own, and I love seeing it pay off for her."

"The crochet thing?" Theo asked.

"Yeah. Did you know she has over 2 million followers on social media? She has over 200, 000 email subscribers and her patterns, when released, crash the online retail sites every time because so many people buy them all at once. She's incredible."

Despite not knowing much about online retailers and the craft realm, he knew it took work to build a faithful clientele and he respected Reesa's platform. "I didn't realize that type of thing was so popular."

"Oh yeah. I remember her teaching herself how to crochet when I was about six. Her first attempts were awful, but she worked at it. She had a vision of giving us a free lifestyle to do whatever we wanted, and she made it happen. It's like she knew she'd be where she is now. I don't know how, but she's always been good at setting a goal and doing whatever it takes to reach it. I haven't figured out what Piney, Arkansas, has to do with anything yet or why we moved here specifically, but I know there's a reason, and sooner or later whatever she's envisioned will come to pass."

"I would think she moved here for the wonderful people." He pointed at himself and Clare grinned.

"You were a bonus." She shoved his shoulder and then gave a contented snicker. "Thanks for being her friend. Usually when we move to a new town, people sort of look down on her for being so young and being my mom. Like they know she was a teen mom and just sort of silently snarl." She squinched up her nose in distaste and widened her eyes as if disgusted.

"We all have our pasts. And we all have lives to keep living. And I don't much care what people think. I'll be friends with whomever I please. I left high school a long time ago; don't see the point in acting like I'm still there. No offense."

"None taken. I get it."

They pulled up the drive towards the cabin, a small silver SUV parked out front. "Who is that?" Clare wondered aloud.

"Jamie," Theo replied. "You'll like her." He turned off the engine as Reesa came rushing out of the house in a whirlwind.

"I'm so sorry!" She hugged Clare. "I've been unpacking and then Jamie came over and I lost track of time. And then I realized, as I saw Theo's truck coming up the drive, that it was 3:45, and wow... I'm a terrible mother."

Clare patted her shoulder. "Go easy on yourself. You're not that bad." Reesa tossed a thumb over her shoulder for Clare to get inside so she could talk to Theo.

"Thanks, Theo. I owe you. I promise I normally don't forget my daughter. I—"

"No need to explain. I didn't mind."

"Want to come inside? Jamie brought us an entire meal for supper later. We were thinking about whipping up some afternoon drinks."

"I need to head back to the garage."

"Oh, right. It's not five yet. Do you get off at five usually?"

"Usually."

"Is today a 'usually' kind of day?"

"Probably."

"Good. Then come back here and eat supper with us. There's plenty and it will be my of saying thank you for picking up Clare."

"There's no need to thank me."

"Okay, then just come over to hang out. Jamie will still be here. It will be fun."

"Reesa—"

"Nope. It's settled. Don't make me call your grandmother," she threatened.

"You realize since I've met you, I've spent more time at this ratty old cabin than my own house."

Reesa waved her hand over herself. "Because you have new friends. Yay you! We'll see you at five." She patted his shoulder and hurried back into the cabin, sounds of Taylor Swift blaring on the stereo sifting outside as the door opened.

Giving in, Theo decided to head to the garage, call it a day, close up, go home and shower, grab Trooper from his place, and then head over to Reesa's. If she wanted him to come over after work, it wasn't going to be until he was good and ready.

CHAPTER FIVE

"I'm in love. I'm just absolutely in love with the both of you." Jamie stood back and admired the wall of yarn tucked into cubbies behind the couch as not only a focal point for the room, but also storage. "To create these beautiful things!" She held a crocheted afghan to her cheek and nuzzled it with a contented sigh. "I want everything I see." She pointed to small granny square crocheted coasters, the colorful rug on the floor, and the throw pillows on the couch. "All of it. How do you do this?" She looked to Reesa in admiration and then to Clare, who sat on the couch crocheting her own project. "I mean, both of you just create, create, create, and then get to live in such a colorful wonderland!" She giggled as Clare held up a spare crochet hook.

"Join us," Clare invited.

Jamie squealed and clapped her hands and plopped on the couch next to Clare to watch her.

"It's not that hard," Clare encouraged as a loud knock shook the front door.

"Must be Theo." Reesa walked from her bedroom carrying two heavy binders laden with some of her former patterns to place on the bottom of her bookshelf beside the couch. She walked to the door and opened it with a welcoming smile. "Party is in here." She motioned over her shoulder as she turned and continued her way to delivering her heavy load to the shelf.

"Hey, Theo!" Jamie enthusiastically waved from the couch and held up her single chain of uneven loops of what looked to be the start of her crocheting adventure. "Look at this place! Don't you just love it?!" Jamie's red curls bounced as she situated herself back into the cushions to continue concentrating.

"Crochet party happening over there. Be careful or you'll be sucked in." Reesa, knelt on the floor by the bookshelf, raised to her feet. She nodded towards the cold beer in his hands. "Finally five."

"Finally," he agreed, though it was half past six. She watched as his eyes soaked in the colorful surroundings, the drab cabin transforming from rustic to bohemian cubby with the added textures and colors of all her crochet work. She and Clare liked living amongst the mismatched and colorful menagerie, but she knew it could be overwhelming to some people. By Theo's quiet appraisal, she could tell he was on the fence. "You've been busy."

"Yeah. It was a full day. And thankfully Jamie kept me company, so I kept moving along. Oh—" She snapped and walked towards the laundry basket he'd brought to them, his linens all folded and stacked neatly inside. "I'm returning these. I washed them for you."

"You didn't have to do that."

"It killed her to do it," Clare called out.

"It did," Reesa admitted. "Now they smell like me instead of clean male."

"Oooooh that's a great smell," Jamie agreed with a bouncy bob of her head.

"Which," Reesa fanned a hand from Theo to herself. "You currently smell like." She inhaled a deep breath and sighed. "Yep, that's it. Clean male."

"You're going to send him running, Mom," Clare warned and shot him an apologetic look for her mom's quirks.

"He's stronger than that." Reesa motioned for him to have a seat in the wing back chair in the living room. "Supper is almost ready. Right, Jamie?"

Jamie flipped her wrist over to glance at her watch. "Yep. Five or so minutes."

A whine and a light scratch tapped the front screen door and Clare glanced up. "Trooper! Hey, boy!" She set her crochet aside and walked to let him in the house, the dog excited to see his new friend.

"I wasn't sure if you wanted him in here now that you're somewhat settled." Theo watched as Clare sat on the rug and Trooper rolled on his back for belly rubs.

"He's always welcome." Reesa took Clare's place on the couch and picked up the project her daughter had been working on, and without glancing at it, began moving her fingers in expert fashion, the shape of brightly colored flower petals coming into view. "So, how was the rest of your day? How's my car?"

"It's still there. Door will be here Wednesday."

"And will you be the one working on it?" Reesa tried to keep her tone casual, but she wanted to make sure Theo was the one entrusted with her vehicle and not Mike. She didn't want to have any interaction with the other man, even briefly. By Theo's expression, and the way Jamie and Clare paused in their different tasks, her tone was anything but casual.

"Do you want someone else?" he asked.

"No. I want it to be you," Reesa confirmed, looking down at her project.

Theo cleared his throat and Reesa briefly glanced up. "Is there a specific reason you want it to be me?" he asked. "My other guys are more than capable."

Great, she thought. *He'd picked up on something being wrong.* She didn't think anything was wrong with the other men's abilities, so how did she convey that without him handing the repair to one of them if he ended up getting busy with something else?

"Reesa—" His eyes narrowed on her, and she shrugged.

"I would just rather you do it, that's all."

"Does this have anything to do with Mike?" he asked.

Her hands fumbled. *How did he know?*

"If it has anything to do with his attraction towards you, I assure you that it won't undermine his work. He's good at what he does."

"Attraction?" Jamie asked with a glimmer of zeal that she coughed back when she saw the dismay on Reesa's face. "Ummm, I mean... how dare he?" she mumbled.

"There is no attraction," Reesa attempted to counter. "He just... rubbed me the wrong way is all. And I would rather my car be in your capable hands than his... well, than his. There. That's all." She locked eyes with Theo, and he gave a curt nod.

"Understood." And without another word on the subject, she knew he'd take care of her car himself. She liked that Theo never pushed for more than she was willing to give. He seemed okay with her vibes or feelings being off and instead of nudging for her to explain, he accepted them as they were, respected them, and went on. For someone who'd just met her, he seemed extremely in tune with her feelings.

"T.J.'s the best, anyway," Jamie complimented. "When we were freshmen in high school, he basically took apart my entire car and put it back together in like a week. And it ran better after he did."

"Any type of maintenance would have helped that car. I did nothing special."

"Liar." Jamie winked at him.

"You two went to high school together?" Clare asked.

Jamie nodded. "We went to school from kindergarten all the way to graduation together."

"Wow." Clare's eyes widened. "That's really cool."

"Ol' T.J. over there was the biggest heartthrob back in the day." Jamie giggled as she embarrassed him.

Clare grinned at him. "What was he like?"

"Oh, he was about like he is now," Jamie continued. "Tall, brooding, mysterious. It had all the girls in a tizzy."

Reesa chuckled but said nothing as she saw Theo uncomfortably shift in his seat at being the topic of conversation.

"Did you date a lot?" Clare asked, shooting her mom a look as if they'd discussed dating multiple times over the years.

"No." Theo shook his head.

"No one was ever good enough for T." Jamie shook her head but then lifted a hand to tease her hair. "Except me."

"What? No way!" Clare smiled. "You two dated?"

Theo's lips quirked as if he were about to smile as Jamie continued mimicking styling herself.

"No. We didn't," Theo clarified.

"But we were prom dates," Jamie continued. "It drove the girls crazy!" She guffawed. "And T.J. was nice enough to take me even though he didn't want to go. I'll have to dig up the pictures and show 'em to you." She winked at Clare.

"Please don't." Theo stood to his feet and walked towards the trash can, which was still a loose trash bag draped on the back of one of the kitchen chairs, and tossed his empty beer can inside. He walked over to the oven and pulled out the two dishes Jamie had covered in foil.

"Oh, shoot!" Jamie snapped her fingers and wriggled off the deep-set sofa to her feet. "Thanks, T. I forgot about those." She hurried towards the small kitchen and lifted the foil, fanning away the steam. Her hip nudged him out of the way as she took over and he made his way back to the living room. Jamie snapped her fingers. "No, you don't, mister. Dishes are in that cabinet. Set the table."

Reesa watched as Theo did Jamie's bidding and withdrew four of her mismatched plates and set them at the small table. He noticed only the three chairs and walked outside the house. He returned with a five-gallon bucket that he turned upside down as the fourth seat. "Remind me to get you a fourth chair."

A horn honked from outside and Theo walked to the door, Reesa not having to get up from the couch. She watched as his shoulders relaxed and she heard Billy Lou greet him. The older woman breezed inside with a brightly painted smile and a welcome embrace for Jamie. Clare hopped to her feet, as did Reesa, setting her project aside.

"Well, look at all of you." She held her hands over her mouth as she gasped and spun around several times. "My goodness, look how beautiful this place is. Reesa, honey, I *love* it." She hugged Reesa, giving her a small back rub with one of her hands before releasing her. "Theodore." She hugged her grandson and tugged on the front of his beard. "Good to see you socializing."

Jamie snorted and then slapped a reassuring hand on Theo's shoulder. "Gotta love it when Mrs. Billy calls it like it is."

"What brings you by, Grandma?" Theo asked.

"I wanted to check up on my girls." She motioned towards Reesa and Clare. "But I see you are taking care of that." Her leading tone had Jamie stifling another giggle with her hand as Theo turned serious eyes on his old friend. "And I see you all are about to eat supper. I was coming by to sweep them away for a Seymore's night out, but I'm too late."

"That would have been wonderful, Billy Lou." Reesa gestured towards the table. "Do you want to join us?"

"Oh, heavens no, sweetie. You all eat. I'm going to head into town anyway. I'll take a rain check, though. Theo, walk me out, honey." She linked her arm with her grandson's and ushered him outside.

"What do you think she's saying to him?" Clare asked, peeking through the curtain to spy.

"Clare Petunia Tate, get back here," Reesa called.

"Petunia?" Jamie asked.

"No," Clare corrected. "She just makes one up each time, but I'm pretty sure my middle name is Emily."

Reesa winked at her daughter.

"She's probably just scolding him about something," Jamie answered their curiosity. "Probably for scowling. That's always been her go-to. Even when T.J. is perfectly fine, she'd always tell him to smile or be kind."

"So far, other than our present company of course," Reesa tilted her head at Jamie. "Theo's been one of the kindest people I've met in a long time."

"Likewise." Clare snuck a bite of pasta from the casserole Jamie placed on the table. "Though Teddy is a close second." Reesa pinned her daughter with a firm look and Clare rolled her eyes. "I don't have a crush on Teddy, Mom. He's just nice and seems like he'll be a good friend."

"I don't know if I believe you, but I'll pretend for now."

"Thank you." Clare hurried away from the window. "He's coming back. He doesn't look happy. Well... he looks less happy than he did before. Does he ever look truly happy?" she asked the room before sliding into one of the empty kitchen chairs and pretending to take a sip of water.

Theo stepped inside and walked over to the table and sat on the bucket.

"Everything alright?" Reesa asked, sensing a darkening of his mood as well.

"Fine." He looked up at Jamie and she hustled into action of finding her own seat and spooning helpings on everyone's plates.

Reesa raised her water glass. "To a new town, a new home, and new friends."

"Woo hoo!" Clare chimed, clinking her glass with Jamie's and then Theo's.

Jamie leaned back in her chair and sighed with a dimpled smile on her face. "I am just so happy for new faces in town and new friends. It's been a while since Piney's gotten any fresh blood. Well, people our age. Right, T?" Theo took a bite of his supper and shrugged. "He doesn't care because everyone is T.J.'s friend." Jamie stirred her fork on her plate before setting it down. "I don't have many friends in Piney," she admitted. "So thank you, Reesa, for inviting me over today."

"You caffeinated me, you've brought me food, and you're sweet to my daughter. Why would I not invite you over?" Reesa tapped her glass to Jamie's for a second time and caught Theo's appreciative glance before he went back to his plate. There was no doubt in her mind that Jamie was an excellent person. And she hated to hear the insecurity in the woman's tone when discussing friendships. But

Reesa understood. She never really took the time to create lasting friendships because she and Clare moved so frequently. But Piney was different. It would be different, she told herself. Because if— and it was a big *if*— *if* she did reach out to her parents in Hot Springs and try to reconnect and it actually went well, then she would want to stay close by... for Clare's sake. And Piney, so far, seemed quaint and quiet enough to do that. She liked quiet places. It allowed her mind to drift and create. And the cabin was a dream, tucked away and shadowed by gorgeous, tall pine trees. Sure, it needed a bit of fixing up, but she liked that about it. She liked taking weathered things and making something beautiful out of them. Most of their belongings were second hand finds that she and Clare breathed new life into. She wasn't afraid to splash a can of paint, bedazzle, or cover up the old to make it new. She liked eclectic, and her house, despite being mismatched, melded together to create a comfortable, safe, and inviting home for her and Clare. And now for Jamie and Theo. They all seemed like misfits in some form or fashion. Jamie, though bubbly and cheerful, sheltered feelings of insecurity from what seemed like years of rejection. Theo, as popular as he may be in town, seemed to want to live in the shadows and not be noticed, and then there was her. Reesa. Single mom. Floater. Coffee addict. She didn't take the time to mentally list all her qualities and titles because she knew them well. Positive and negative, she'd heard them all over the years. She was used to being the misfit, and at times, the outcast. She didn't want that for Clare. She'd strived and worked as hard as she was capable of to ensure that her daughter never felt that way. And so far, Clare seemed above it all. Her daughter was as every teen should be: carefree and loved. Reesa failed and flopped at so many things as a mom, but instead of letting the guilt eat at her over the years, she adapted, learned, and moved on so that Clare became a chameleon too and did the same. Growth took time. And it wasn't impossible. Maybe, just maybe, she wasn't the only one to grow over the years. Maybe her parents had too. All she could do was hope, because as she looked at her daughter laughing and acting out comedy skits with Jamie that made even the serious Theo chuckle in his seat, Reesa knew she didn't want to leave Piney. She wanted this to be her home. She wanted these people to be her friends. And she wanted her daughter to have a relationship with her grandparents. *Maybe it could happen.*

~

Theo left Reesa's with not only a small plastic container of leftovers, but an easy stride. It'd been a nice evening. Though Jamie had shared rather embarrassing stories from their high school days, he found it fun to reminisce and to laugh at his younger self. He'd grown up a lot since high school. Life didn't go the direction he'd planned. He was going to play college ball, maybe professionally, but he'd never considered staying in his hometown. The thought hadn't even been on his radar. But life happens, plans change, futures change, and his took a turn he hadn't expected. He made the best of it. He liked owning his auto repair shop. He liked living in the woods. He liked having the extra years of living near his grandparents, especially since losing his grandfather. He and Billy Lou had a unique relationship because of the direction his life headed, and he wouldn't change it. He was closer to his grandmother than his own parents, and he valued that relationship. When she'd shown up at Reesa's, he'd anticipated her hanging around, but appreciated that she didn't. Her curiosity was no doubt killing her as to why he was there, but he'd let her stew over it. He smiled to himself, happy that he could still surprise her after all these years. He could be social, when he wanted to be, but her facial expression at seeing him at Reesa's was almost priceless.

And then she'd told him about the prowler. His smile slipped from his face as he tried to think of what precautions to take regarding Reesa and Clare. The old cabin had no fancy alarm system, and even though he left Trooper there, under the guise that the dog had missed Clare, he knew his dog could do nothing against a determined stranger barging inside. He already decided he'd camp outside in his truck at the edge of the yard. He didn't want to scare Reesa, so he planned to park it there in a couple of hours when he knew she and Clare were asleep. He'd keep an eye on the place for the night. His grandmother assured him she would be fine. Not long after his grandfather's death, Billy Lou had installed a state-of-the-art alarm system that a leaf could set off if it blew too close to the sensor. She also knew how to handle herself in emergency situations. Well, more like handle the single shot twelve-gauge shotgun that had belonged to his grandfather. But Billy Lou wasn't overly dramatic either. When she'd mentioned her trash cans being rummaged through and the garage door being tampered with, Theo knew she was telling the truth.

He had no idea if Reesa owned a weapon. Knowing her, she'd blare her stereo into the night and not hear a sound should someone come prowling. He deposited his leftovers into his refrigerator and went ahead and took his shower. By the time he'd gathered his own shotgun and a thermos of coffee, he considered it dark enough to make the drive to Reesa's to keep watch. He hadn't mentioned his grandmother's warning because he didn't want to frighten Reesa or Clare, but especially Clare. The teen had already expressed nervousness about a new place, and he didn't want her to think this was a common occurrence. She'd never sleep easy otherwise. He climbed into his pickup and drove the bumpy, darkened dirt path towards the cabin. He didn't jostle too much because he knew this path better than anyone. He'd grown up riding up and down this dirt road. He and his brother would camp in the cabin with his grandfather most of the summer, riding four-wheelers, fishing, and swimming in the pond. He killed his headlights as he approached the cabin and pulled towards the tree line. He rolled his windows down and turned off the engine. Thankfully, the temperature wasn't too stifling. That would hit in a couple of months, but for now, the night was pleasant and quiet. The only sound was the breeze whistling through the tall pines. Peaceful, relaxing, home. He exhaled and relaxed his shoulders as he shifted into a comfortable slouch in his seat. Now he waited and watched. He didn't anticipate any problems, but the risk of the two women inside being faced with an invader was too bothersome for him to just let it slide for the night. Plus, Billy Lou would never let him hear the end of it if he didn't do *something* to help. She'd raised him better than that. And it was in his nature to want to help. He didn't mind helping folks. It was part of what made Piney a great place to live. People saw about one another here. And the new tenants in his grandmother's cabin fell underneath his realm of responsibility. He bet Reesa would balk at the thought of a man stepping in to protect her when she hadn't asked for it, but it was who he was. She didn't have to ask. And if he wanted to be honest with himself, he'd admit that he had a soft spot for her and her daughter. He wanted them to feel safe and secure. He wanted Clare to have a home that lasted longer than a year or two. He wasn't sure why it bothered him that she hadn't had that in her life, but it did. Every kid deserved to have a place they called home. A place that brought them peace and feelings of warmth when thought about. He'd had that for the most part growing up. His parents provided a wonderful life for him and his siblings. Until he'd become a disappointment to his father. Then Billy Lou stepped in and gave him what he needed. He lived his senior year of high school with his grandparents, and he never once felt like a burden or nuisance. They loved him. Despite him not going to college on scholarship, despite him not pursuing college in general, and despite his many failures, his grandparents loved him. Unconditionally. Every kid needed a Billy Lou in their life.

A rustling sound caught his attention and he straightened in his seat, leaning partially out of his open window. A scuffle and scrape sounded from the back porch and Theo quietly exited his truck, shotgun in hand. He tiptoed to the side of the house so as to sneak up on the intruder. He'd just stepped onto the porch, when a scruffy head peaked over the side of Reesa's trashcan. He lowered his gun and clicked the safety in place, walking quietly towards the raggedy raccoon. When he was even with the back entrance of the cabin, the door swung open, and a banshee-screaming Reesa emerged brandishing a baseball bat and pepper spray. She sprayed and swung without thought and Theo felt the painful sting hit his eyes and gasped. He held up a hand to defend himself as the baseball bat landed a hard swing to his bicep. He grunted and swatted his hand in the darkness to try and grab it. Reesa continued her attack until he finally snatched the bat from her hands and tossed it into the yard. "It's me!" His voice was hoarse from the cloud of pepper spray that he'd endured. "Reesa, it's me." Her advance stopped, and her heavy breaths of exertion had him moving his hand until he felt her head and hair. He slid his hand to her shoulder, his eyes blind with spray and darkness.

"Theo?" Her whisper was harsh and loud against the quiet. "What are you doing here? I thought you were a burglar."

"Raccoon." He felt her hand rest upon his on her shoulder, her grip jittery as she squeezed his fingers. "Reesa, I can't see."

"Oh geez." Reesa rested her forehead briefly against the side of his arm. "Come on." She removed his gun from his other hand and rested it against the wall of the cabin and then draped both his hands on her shoulders as she guided him into the house. "Quiet. We're passing Clare's room," she whispered, leading him down the hall towards the kitchen. She removed his right hand and placed it on the counter's edge, and he began clumsily searching for the sink. He knocked a bottle of soap over and it fell to the floor with a thud. "Shhh!" Reesa hissed. "I'll help you, just hold on a second." She flicked a light on, and he tried to open his eyes, but the pain was too much to bear. He groaned as he hunched over and rested his head on his arms.

She nudged him over and he heard the tap come to life. "Lean your head down." She began to splash water on his face, and he followed suit. It wasn't instant relief, but it helped, the cooling sensation allowing him to blink away tears and more of the burn. His skin felt on fire, and he wasn't sure how long the pain would last. He smelled the spray in his beard and grabbed the soap bottle off the floor and pumped ample amounts into his hand and washed his face and beard as best he could. He felt a hand towel being shoved into his hand and he patted his face dry. He blinked, the sting still there, but bearable. "You alright?" He turned and Reesa flinched at his appearance.

"That bad, huh?"

"It's pretty bad. I'm sorry. I thought you were... well, we already established that. But I wasn't expecting you. I mean, why were you even here?"

"Billy Lou had signs of a prowler at her house and asked that I keep an eye on you two tonight just in case."

"A prowler?" Reesa's voice trembled with fear.

"Don't worry, I think we found him. That raccoon is your prowler. Though he got away."

"I doubt he'll be back after a crazy woman almost killed him and her rescuer." She stifled a giggle and then patted his arm. He grunted and hissed at the soreness of where she'd hit him with the baseball bat. "Oh, right, oops. I'm so sorry, Theo. I'll get you some ice. Why don't you have a seat on the sofa?"

He didn't have to be asked twice. Miserably, he found a seat and leaned his head back closing his eyes. He felt a cold washcloth rest over his eyelids, and he grunted in appreciation as an ice pack was applied to his arm and Reesa gently wound a cloth around his bicep to hold it in place. "That's going to be sore and will probably bruise."

"Mmhmm." Her hands stilled after she tucked the tail end of the towel wrap into itself. He knew she hadn't gotten up off the sofa because the cushion hadn't shifted yet. He held out a hand, palm up and she gently rested her small hand in his. He gave it a reassuring squeeze before releasing it. "Sorry to scare you."

"You definitely did," Reesa admitted. "But I appreciate the heroics."

"Wasted heroics, you mean."

"Are you upset you didn't get to save the night?" she asked with a touch of humor in her tone. "Absolutely. What man wouldn't be?"

He felt a light flutter on his cheek as she kissed him. "My hero. That better?"

"It'll suffice."

She chuckled softly and her leg brushed his as she shifted on the sofa. He knew she watched him, but he couldn't bring himself to remove his eye covering just yet. The burn lingered for another ten minutes before it began to fade. Reesa's head rested upon his shoulder. When he did remove his cold compress, Reesa was sound asleep against him. A throat cleared and his gaze landed on Clare's at the edge of the hallway. He shifted, hoping she didn't think he was here in the middle of the night calling upon her mother. When he scooted to rise to his feet, Reesa's head bobbed, and she snapped awake. "Sorry, I fell asleep. Wait- What are you doing? You can't drive yet."

"I feel much better. I can just walk home. I'll get my truck in the morning."

"Theo, wait, you can't just walk through the woods in the middle of the night. A coyote could get you or something."

"I'll be fine. I'll have my shotgun."

"Mom?" Clare asked. "What's going on?"

Sighing, Reesa thread her hand through her hair. "I thought we had someone trying to break in, but it was a raccoon, and Theo was here to capture it, but I thought he was the bad guy, so I beat the snot out of him and bathed him with pepper spray."

Clare's hand covered her mouth as she tried not to laugh, and she nodded with wide eyes at Theo's condition. "Oh."

"I'll give you one laugh," Theo muttered, as he walked past her towards the back of the cabin to head out the way he'd come. He heard a light giggle escape from the girl, and he couldn't help but smirk at the predicament as well. He made sure his stony façade was back in place before turning back around to Reesa as she stepped out on the porch with him. She crossed her arms over the crop top she wore, the short pajama shorts catching his eye before he reached for his gun. "I'll see you tomorrow at some point, I'm sure."

"Theo, I really am sorry I went all Resident Evil on you."

"I don't even know what that means."

"Alice. You know, zombie killer? What am I saying? Of course you don't know. You're you. We seriously need to get started on that pop culture education of yours, Theo."

"Maybe when I can actually see." He rested his gun on his shoulder and began walking to the edge of the woods, Reesa in step beside him. He paused and she waited patiently with her hands on her hips, her exposed midrift forgotten. "I'm not leavin' until you're inside that cabin." He looked down at her and she hesitated a moment. He could tell she fought against the urge to quip something else his way, but her eyes were serious as she nodded and gave him a friendly pat on the shoulder that slid down his arm to his hand. She squeezed before releasing him and scurrying back towards the porch. He couldn't see her, but he heard the door squeak open and closed, and that satisfied him enough to have him stumbling home.

CHAPTER SIX

Reesa appreciated Billy Lou giving her a lift to town. She had to talk to Jamie about last night's encounter with Theo. She hadn't seen him yet and noticed his truck was gone before Teddy had come to pick Clare up from school. Therefore, her only ticket to town was his grandmother. Reesa immediately confessed her blunder on the off-chance Billy Lou had already spoken to her grandson and knew Reesa had whipped him with a baseball bat.

"Oh my goodness!" Billy Lou wiped a tear from her eye as she hooted in laughter at Reesa's retelling. "Bless his heart. He was probably cursin' me for having him keep watch." She slapped a hand on the steering wheel as she laughed and turned into the parking lot of Java Jamie. "I'll have to go check on him and see how he's doing." She patted Reesa's leg. "Honey, you have brought more excitement to his life in the last week than he's had in years."

"I'm sure he doesn't see it as a good thing after last night," Reesa admitted. "Please, when you see him, tell him I'm sorry again, won't you?"

"Oh, of course. You don't feel bad about nothin', sweetie. It was an accident, and Theodore's tough. He can handle it. Now, you enjoy time with Jamie and your crochet. I'll swing by about three to pick you up."

"Thank you again for being my chauffeur."

"Honey, I live for it." Billy Lou beamed as she waited for Reesa to gather her project bag, purse, and cell phone and stepped out.

"Let me know if he needs anything. I owe him." Reesa shut her door as Billy Lou sped away in the direction of Theo's garage. She was tempted to ride over there with her, but she didn't want to embarrass him. She also wasn't sure if she was ready to see him after last night. She opened the door to the coffee shop, and Jamie's head popped up from behind the counter.

"Hey-O! If it's not Louisville Slugger!"

Reesa's jaw dropped. "You already know? How?"

Jamie bent over with a hearty laugh. "T.J. was in this morning. Girl, you've got a swing on you." She pointed to her arm and made circling motions. "He's got a bruise the size of Africa."

Reesa palmed her forehead and Jamie waved away her shame. "Trust me. He wears it with pride. He's a man; that kind of thing makes them feel all good and stuff."

"Not Theo."

She shrugged. "I don't know. He seemed okay to me, though. A little on the self-conscious side, but that's to be expected."

"I already feel bad," Reesa reminded her friend. "Me impacting his confidence doesn't make me feel any better."

"Girl, not you." Jamie giggled. "He- wait. You haven't seen him this morning?"

"No. Why?"

"Ah." Jamie wriggled her eyebrows. "I'm not going to spoil it. You'll see him soon enough, I'm sure. Now, what can I get ya?"

"Anything with caffeine." Reesa motioned towards a fluffy sofa. "Can I set up shop today?"

"Of course." Jamie waved her on. "I'll bring it over and we'll start you a tab."

"Sounds good." Reesa walked to the couch and set her bags down. She fished her earbuds out of her purse and set her phone to play an audiobook as she began working on her latest pattern project. She configured a few stitches and noted them down in her notebook. She gave a nod of thanks to Jamie when she set a frothy, whipped topping-covered drink in front of her. For hours she sat and worked, losing track of time. She took a break for lunch to have leftover quiches with Jamie before picking up her crochet hook and getting back to work. She'd planned to launch a new pattern for a vintage granny square cardigan by the end of the month and was hoping to film a few training videos over the next couple of days when she reached the section on attaching the sleeves to the main body. The income from a new pattern launch would give her the extra money for them to buy a new television. She and Clare had decided that upon this latest move, that that would be their next investment. They enjoyed watching movies together. It was their favorite thing to do besides crochet, and the fact they could do both at the same time was even better. Reesa hoped to take Clare to a movie in Hot Springs on Friday night in celebration of her first completed week of school.

Maybe Jamie and Theo would want to join them, if Theo would even still talk to her after her assault. She dreaded seeing him. He'd been nothing but nice, and she'd attacked him. If she'd just paid attention last night before swinging and spraying, all of this could have been avoided. But no, she was a lunatic and she hit first, asked questions later. Yes, she was scared, and her adrenaline was pumping, but she didn't even pause to acknowledge who the prowler could have been before launching into attack mode. If she had, Theo would have been spared, and their next encounter wouldn't be awkward, and she'd still have her new friend. She doubted he wanted to hang around the cabin now that she'd gone crazy on him. She wouldn't sulk, though. She wasn't a sulker. She liked Theo. She liked his socially awkward behavior and scowl, and she liked that he didn't quite fit in, nor did he want to. She'd hoped to become better friends with him, but she would have to accept the fact he didn't want to be now. It was just the rules of the game. You beat someone with a baseball bat and almost blind them, they don't have to be your friend. It was only fair. She didn't like the fact that her heart sank at the thought of him dismissing her. But again, he had every right.

A wadded-up napkin pelted against her temple, and she looked up to see Billy Lou sitting next to her with brightly colored lips smiling. Reesa paused her audiobook and removed her earbuds. "I'm sorry, I didn't realize it was already time."

"It's not." Billy Lou pointed as Mike, the mechanic from Theo's garage, stood with a pair of keys in his hands.

"I come bearing gifts." He flashed his devilish grin and she saw Jamie feign a swoon behind the counter before she reached for them.

"Thank you."

"You're welcome. Boss said he'd swing by later to make sure it ran to your liking, but he was swamped at the garage and asked me to deliver it to you."

Billy Lou waved him away. "Thanks, Mikey. You take care now."

He tipped his head in a slight bow, winked at Reesa, and left.

"He gets me every time in those tight jeans," Jamie called, several customers laughing at her comment.

Reesa rolled her eyes and Billy Lou patted her knee. "Theo saw you over here and thought you might like to have your wheels back." Billy Lou squinted at her. "What's the matter, honey? You don't seem that excited."

"She is. She's just bummed T.J. didn't come himself," Jamie butted in, and Reesa denied the charge.

"Not so."

"Girl, it is written all over you." Jamie giggled as she swiped a towel under the condensation rings of Reesa's cup on the side table and set it on a coaster.
Billy Lou's brows lifted into her hairline at the obvious truth to Jamie's statement.

"It's not what you're thinking," Reesa clarified. "The both of you." She pointed at the two women. "I'm just not wanting him to be upset with me or feel like I'm too whackadoo to be around now. I mean, I really let it fly last night when I went into Mama Bear mode protecting my house."

"Which is to be expected." Billy Lou patted her thigh. "Theodore understands that. Besides, his grumps today have nothing to do with last night's shenanigans. It has to do with change. He despises change."

"What change, though?" Reesa held up her hands as Billy Lou and Jamie exchanged amused glances.

"Why don't you see for yourself." Jamie nodded towards the front window as Theo reached for the door handle to walk inside. When he cleared the threshold, Reesa gasped, her crochet hook falling from her fingers.

"Oh. My." She whispered, as the other two women bit back grins. Theo's serious eyes found hers and he purposefully walked her direction. "You get your keys from Mike?"

She nodded, eyes wide.

"Good. I'm sorry I had to have him bring them to you, but it was the only way I could get them to you before 3:30 just in case you had to pick up Clare today. I've got to head back. I only had a few minutes, but I wanted to apologize just in case Mike... well, I know you don't prefer to deal with him." He rushed and then paused on a bated breath, his hands on his hips. "What is it?"

Reesa stood and walked towards him, her eyes drilling into his. Theo shifted on his feet as if to flee at any moment before her fingers lifted to lightly brush against his bare chin and cheeks. "Wow." Her eyes, full of wonder, turned towards the other women. "This is what was hiding under that grubby beard?"

The other two women nodded with amused expressions and Theo gently slapped her hands away. "Okay, I've got to go." He turned to leave, and Reesa tugged on his arm with a laugh.

"Theo, wait, I just want to see you."

"No thanks. I've been stared at all day. Don't need to be a spectacle when I have work to do."

"At least let me see your arm." Reesa knew she'd won when his retreat halted, and he relaxed. She lifted his sleeve and grimaced. "Yikes. I did that."

"Yes, you did."

Reesa looked up at him again, her eyes transfixed on the transformation a clean shave brought to his face. Theo had been handsome before, in a rugged sort of way. Now, he was just flat out gorgeous, and her heart did a small flip when his dark, uncertain eyes landed on her.

"You're staring again," he mumbled.

Reesa blinked. "I'm sorry. I don't mean to. You just... look different. A good different, don't get me wrong. Just... different. Your eyes are still red." She lifted her hand and he flinched before she even touched him.

"Sorry, my skin is still sensitive. Kind of hurts."

"Got it. Don't touch." Reesa lightly ran the back of her knuckle down his smooth cheek. "Sorry. I had to get one last one in. You have to come show Clare later. She won't believe it."

"I'd rather not show off my shaved face, thank you."

"Why not? It's nice," Reesa complimented. "Like, really nice. Did you forget what you looked like underneath?"

"Okay, I'm leaving. I was in a hurry, and in your usual fashion, you've derailed this entire conversation."

"Right. Well, you should still swing by later to show Clare. Otherwise, we're going to come bug you at your house so she can see."

He huffed in annoyance on his way to the door. "Did it ever occur to you that I might have plans this evening that don't involve you? Maybe I'm busy and can't swing by. Or maybe I'll have company and don't want visitors."

Reesa crossed her arms over her chest and surveyed him with an amused stare. He wilted instantly. "Fine. Whatever. You're going to do what you want anyway."

"You know me well already. Ha, there it is, the familiar Theo scowl. I was wondering what it'd look like now." She flashed a chummy grin.

"I'll come by after work." Avoiding her last remark, he stalked out, the door closing roughly behind him.

Reesa spun around and clapped her hands in success. "Clare is going to flip when she sees him. Wow, he looks so different. I mean, not too different, the same Theo is there. But yeah, wow, Billy Lou. You didn't tell me he was such a hunk."

"I did," Jamie pointed out. "I specifically remember telling you he was the heartthrob back in the day."

"Back in the day, sure," Reesa added. "But not now? What's up with that? That man is... perfection."

Billy Lou laughed. "I'm glad you think so, honey. I think it's his warm and fuzzy personality that keeps people at a distance."

Reesa and Jamie guffawed at the older woman's sarcasm. "Yeah, I guess he is a bit prickly most of the time," Reesa admitted. "But it's part of his charm. We had him laughing the other night, didn't we, Jamie?"

"We did. It was good to see, Billy Lou. T.J. really loosened up and relaxed."

"I'm glad to hear it. And I'm glad you're pestering him." She nudged Reesa's shoulder. "It's good for him. Maybe it'll give him some of his confidence back and he'll put himself out there more. That boy has lived in the woods all by himself for far too long. He needs some good friends to come shake him up."

"I'm good at that," Reesa declared.

"Honey, I can already see that." Billy Lou lifted to her feet. "Alright, I'm heading to Hot Springs for a fundraiser dinner this evening. Jamie, sweetie, are you still my date?"

"Yes ma'am. I've got my black chiffon dress hanging at the ready."

"Perfect. I'll pick you up at seven. Reesa, sweetie, you get 'im, girl." She winked at her before seeing herself out.

"I want to be her when I grow up." Reesa admitted.

"Yep." Jamie agreed. "And I'm pretty sure she just gave you the go ahead to date her grandson."

Reesa blanched. "What?"

"She just told you to 'get 'im,' didn't she?" Jamie snickered.

"Well, yeah, but she meant bug him, not date him."

"Don't you want to?"

"No." Reesa shook her head, her eyes wide with fear.

Jamie paused in gathering up abandoned cups. "Really?"

"Yes, really. I don't want to date Theo. I just want to be his friend."

"Seriously?" Jamie asked. "Even after all your comments about how handsome he is?"

"I can think he's handsome without dating him," Reesa admitted.

"Yeah, but-"

"But what?" Reesa began stuffing her yarn into her work bag, her hands fumbling with her crochet hook as she unzipped its carrier and stuffed it inside. "I don't date."

"Why not?"

"Because I don't." Reesa's voice sounded panicked, and Jamie held up her hands as a sign of surrender, concern etched on her face.

"Okay. I guess I just misunderstood."

"I've got to get home. Clare will be coming home in a few minutes from school." Reesa shouldered her bags. "Thanks for letting me work here today." She handed a stack of bills to Jamie to cover her tab, her new friend perplexed at her overreaction towards their conversation. She knew she needed to calm down, but at the moment, she just wanted to get home. "I'll see ya tomorrow."

"Okay." Jamie's face fell, as if she felt like Reesa was dismissing her as well, and Reesa knew the woman struggled with her own demons of rejection.

"Look, I... I've never had much luck with relationships," Reesa admitted. "Most people snub me once they find out I was an unwed teen mother and have never married. It comes with a lot of rejection." She caught Jamie's understanding gaze. "It's easier to avoid that all together and just not date. I don't plan to date Theo. I honestly just like him and would like to be his friend."

"Noted." Jamie nodded. "I won't tease you about it."

"Thanks for understanding."

"Hey, if anyone knows about being rejected, it's me." Jamie pointed at herself. "I mean, my hot date tonight is a woman in her seventies."

Reesa grinned. "Hey, a night out with Billy Lou is probably one of the best dates a girl could ask for."

"I'm countin' on it." Jamie giggled in her usual upbeat manner. "I'll text you a picture of my dress once I'm all done up."

"Deal. See ya later." Stepping outside, Reesa liked that she and Jamie parted ways in better spirits and with clarification on the Theo situation. There was no denying Reesa was attracted to him. Who wouldn't be? But she had learned over the years that even the most down-to-earth, understanding of men still had issues with her past. At first, they seemed fine, until they met her teenage daughter, and then it was as if reality would hit them, and they freaked out and ran. Every. Single. Time. She didn't want to attempt anything with Theo and then have him back out like all the rest had. At this point, he was one of her only two friends in Piney, and Clare loved the guy. Him distancing himself from them because they tried and failed at a relationship would hurt Clare. And Reesa would do anything to prevent her daughter from feeling the hurt that comes from rejection. Reesa was used to it; she had dealt with rejection most of her life. But

KATHARINE E. HAMILTON

her daughter, Reesa vowed, would never have to feel that way if she could help it. And in this instance, she could. Theo was her friend. Period.

He'd shower first. After a long day, it was the first thing on his mind when he thought of home. A shower, then a beer, then a walk in the garden. After that, he could go over to Reesa's. His eyes were no longer burning from the night before, and his skin had returned to its natural color. He was sad to see the beard go, but he could not wash out the smell of the pepper spray no matter how much he tried. He'd felt awkward all day; already being teased by the boys at work, then Billy Lou, then Jamie... and then Reesa. Well, she hadn't teased him, but she stared at him, and that made him feel weird too. It's not like he was a stranger to any of them, but you would have thought they'd never seen him before. He turned onto his driveway and groaned as soon as he saw Trooper. Trooper had been at Reesa's, which meant one thing... Reesa and Clare were at his house. When he rounded the curve of his tree-lined drive, sure enough, Reesa and Clare sat on his front deck stairs. His house, built similarly to the small cabin they occupied, had a wraparound wooden porch that stretched out into a deck in the front and back to allow for entertaining, though he didn't really utilize it for that. Instead, he had some containers holding his tomato plants along the porches to save space in his garden for other plants. He pulled to a stop, Trooper greeting him with excitement. He took a moment, observing the two female occupants seated on his front steps. He wasn't sure how he felt until he saw Reesa rise to her feet and walk his direction and his pulse kicked up a slight notch. "Not good," he mumbled to himself, wishing away any sort of attraction for the beautiful woman headed his way.

"It's almost six, I was beginning to think you'd chickened out." Reesa appeared next to his truck and narrowed her eyes on him.

"Just getting home."

"I can see that. Now I feel kind of bad about invading your space."

"If you give me about fifteen minutes to shower off this grease and sweat, then I'll forgive you."

"Sure thing." Reesa walked with him towards his porch. "I like your house, by the way."

"Thanks."

Clare stood when he approached. "Whoa."

"Told ya." Reesa placed a proud hand on Theo's shoulder.

Theo smirked. "Okay, get a good look. It *is* because of your mother that I had to shave my beard off."

"Me?" Reesa asked.

"Yes, you." He poked her side with his finger, and she jumped. "That pepper spray would not come out of it."

Reesa nibbled her bottom lip to keep from smiling.

"You look good," Clare complimented. "Not as scary." She motioned a serial killer hacking motion.

Theo looked down at Reesa in surprise at her daughter's comment and Reesa laughed. "She comes by it honest. Don't be offended."

Theo sighed and headed towards his front door, Reesa and Clare remaining on his porch. "You can come inside," he offered.

"We're good." Reesa pointed at Trooper. "We'll play with Trooper for a bit." He nodded and headed into his house.

"It's hot out here, Mom." Clare pointed to the door. "Why did you not want to go in?"

"It's his house. I don't want to intrude any more than we already have."

"Since when do you care about intruding?" Clare asked.

"I've always cared."

"Not with Theo."

"Well, maybe I do now." Reesa threw a tennis ball for Trooper and the dog leapt off the porch in pursuit.

"Do you like him or something?" Clare asked, her tone casual.

"No. Not in the way you mean."

"Why not?"

"What do you mean, why not?"

"He's nice. And really good looking. He tolerates your quirkiness."

"And he's known me a week. Not even a week. Five days. And we've only known him that long as well."

"So?"

"So? Clare, you can't determine if you like someone after only five days. It takes time. And besides, I'm not interested in dating anyone."

"You never are. Well, you are, but you won't because you're terrified they won't like me."

"What?" Reesa turned to her daughter, stunned. Theo, inside the door, stood quietly and listened. He hadn't meant to eavesdrop, but he was surprised they hadn't come in as well and knew Reesa would explain why... and he wanted to know her reasoning.

"You never date because you're worried the guy won't like me. Well, newsflash, Theo has already met me. And I think he likes me. He's smiled, sort of, twice, when we've hung out, so I think that's a pretty good sign coming from him."

Theo smirked at her comment. He did like Clare. She was a cool kid. He was glad she knew he didn't mind having her around.

"There's more to it than that," Reesa added. "Besides, I don't want to date Theo. We just moved here. I don't think it would be wise to date our landlord's grandson. If it didn't work out, which it wouldn't, then it would be an uncomfortable situation for everyone. And then we'd have to move."

"We will anyway in like a year. Might as well go for it." Clare punched her arm in an onward motion and Theo could hear the hurt in Reesa's response.

"I'm sorry we've moved so much over the years."

"Mom, I didn't say it to make you feel guilty. I'm totally fine with how we've lived our lives. I just meant that you could take the risk because if it didn't work out, we wouldn't have to deal with it once we move. We'd just move and move on."

Not hearing any more of their conversation, Theo walked to his room and showered. When he emerged ten minutes later, he heard them in his backyard clearly continuing their conversation about Reesa and himself and her nomadic lifestyle.

"Look at this!" Reesa pointed. "The man is growing corn. Corn!"

"And cucumbers!" Clare's voice held amazement. "How does he do this?"

"He's a wizard. That has to be it. We live next door to Albus Dumbledore, and we had no idea. Maybe we should plant a garden," Reesa suggested. "Could be fun to learn something new."

"And do what with the vegetables? You don't cook."

"Maybe I would, if I grew them myself."

"Highly doubtful."

Unoffended, Reesa continued walking the rows. "I wonder what this one is; sure has pretty leaves and flowers."

"It's potatoes." Theo's voice had Reesa snapping to attention.

"We're admiring your gardening skills." Clare studied her mom a moment before emerging from amongst his plants. "Mom's blown away that you grow and cook with what is here."

"I didn't say that." Reesa admonished her daughter and then mumbled the same thing to Theo. "I didn't say that."

He grinned. "Well, maybe I can show you both how I cook with these. Pick something and we'll whip it up for supper."

"Seriously?" Clare looked impressed and amused at the idea and then she caught her mom's dismissive glance. "Oh, I forgot. Mom and I were going to go to the movies in Hot Springs tonight."

"Reschedule." Theo looked at Reesa and waited until her eyes met his. "It's not every day I offer to cook for someone, and if you go to the movies tomorrow afternoon it will be cheaper because then you can catch the matinee."

"He speaks sense, this one." Clare's hopeful eyes landed on her mom once again and Theo found himself actually looking forward to cooking for company.

"It's a sweet offer, Theo, but we were just here so Clare could see your face. An intrusion upon your dinner plans was not intended."

"What dinner plans? I have none."

"You told me today that I shouldn't assume you didn't."

"So you automatically assume I do?"

She growled. "Well, which is it then? Stop confusing me. I'm trying to be respectful, because you seemed put out with me earlier, and now you're all 'Hey, eat with me. I'm Mr. Cool and Easygoing, and I have this beautiful smile I've been hiding for a decade.' I'm at a loss."

Surprised by her annoyance, Theo crossed his arms and studied her. He saw her eyes flash to the bruise on his arm that peeked out from beneath his sleeve. Guilt covered her face for putting such a mark there. He reached out and nudged her chin with his knuckles until she looked at him again. "Give it up, Tate. You're eating here tonight. And I'll have you know, I've only had that beard the last eight years, not a decade. You guys can even introduce me to whatever pop culture movie you want." Wariness washed over her face and Theo took a cautious step away from her. "If you want."

"Mom, seriously, he's offering supper from some of these cool plants."

Theo chuckled at her statement as he handed Clare his empty metal bucket. "Fill 'er up while your mom is being difficult, I'll fire up the grill for some steaks."

"Fill it up?" Clare asked. "But I don't know what to pick."

"Whatever you want." Theo reached towards Reesa and she hopped away from his touch. "What is the matter, Reesa?" he asked, his tone quiet as he turned his back towards Clare to give them a bit more privacy. "You've been weird since this afternoon. Did I offend you somehow?"

"What? No. Absolutely not. You're like, Mr. Perfect. I doubt offending anyone is in your nature." Reesa stuffed her hands in her back pockets and watched her daughter curiously check out various vegetables and pluck a few here and there.

"Then what is it?" Theo asked, stepping towards her.

Her eyes nervously flashed up to his. "You're just... being all nice and it's weirding me out."

"I've been nice to you since you moved here."

"Well, yeah, but you've always been a little grumpy. Now you're just all friendly and chatty and smiley. When did you want to start talking so much? Or smile even? It's just weird. Especially after I beat you up last night."

He crossed his arms over his broad chest, and he noticed her eyes flash towards the bruise once again. "You feel bad still?"

"Theo, look at your arm." Reesa pointed at the darkened skin. The blue and black smear across his skin was swollen and sore, but he'd had worse over the years. "I did that to you. Me. I'm a horrible human being."

He could tell she believed it of herself. The thought of leaving such a mark on someone obviously haunted her. He lowered his arms and stepped towards her, gently taking both her hands in his. He tugged her towards him and wrapped her arms around his waist and then encircled her with his own. She rested her head against his chest, and he liked the feel of her snugly tucked

KATHARINE E. HAMILTON

against him. Clearing his throat, he released her and stepped away. "There. Better?"

"A little."

"I'm no Vin Diesel, but hey, it was a hug. I don't usually hug. That should count for something."

Her lips parted and she finally flashed her familiar smile. "It does. Thank you for trying to make me feel less like a jerk for injuring you."

"You can make it up to me by helping your daughter pick vegetables to go with tonight's dinner."

"You don't have to feed us, Theo."

"I want to." He narrowed his eyes on her and he watched as she nervously fidgeted with her hair and tucked it behind her ear.

"Alright, then I'm going to introduce you to an American classic tonight. I'll run over to the house and get it."

"Sounds like a plan." He watched as she stopped and whispered something to Clare, her daughter bursting into laughter at her mom's idea and quickly agreeing to it. Clare watched her mom dart through the woods on the well-worn path between the cabin and Theo's house before turning to face him. She walked over and handed him the pail, her smile widening.

"Let's talk about you and my mom."

He rubbed a hand over his mouth and chin before nodding towards the grill. "Then let's do it while I cook."

The teen readily agreed, Trooper falling into step with them as Clare took a seat on the deck and Theo, dreading what she could possibly want to discuss, headed to his refrigerator to grab the steaks. A deep breath later, he headed back outside to face the interrogation of a fifteen-year-old teenage girl.

CHAPTER SEVEN

"*So, you and my mom* are friends, right?" Clare asked, taking a seat in one of his deck chairs as Theo prepped her vegetable medley for the grill.

"I guess. We just met, but sure, I'd say we're becoming friends," Theo acknowledged.

"My mom has a tendency to overshare... about anything."

"I've noticed."

Clare smirked at his response and continued to watch as he shucked three ears of corn and pulled the silks from the kernels. "The one area she seems to be tight-lipped about is her past. Like, before me." Clare explained. "She never mentions much about my grandparents or her life before I came along." Theo didn't respond so she continued. "Has she said anything to you about it?"

"I barely know her, why would she tell me anything she wouldn't tell you?"

"Because you're an adult, and, as we've established, her new friend."

"I'd think she'd feel more comfortable talking to Jamie about that sort of thing at this point." Reaching for a cutting board and knife, she watched as he added the other random vegetables she'd chosen and began chopping them and adding them to a plastic storage bag mixed with olive oil and spices.

"She hasn't mentioned anything? Like, about her parents?" He remained silent and Clare could see his shoulders tighten just a smidgen. "She has, then."

"I didn't say that," Theo replied.

"You didn't have to. Your body language said it all. What did she tell you?"

Sighing, Theo sealed the plastic bag and began shaking the vegetables to evenly coat them in his spice mixture. "It's not for me to tell. Our conversation was, well, ours. I'm sure if she wanted you to know about it, she would have told you."

"So now you know more about my grandparents than I do. Awesome." Clare's aggravation had him setting the vegetables aside and sitting in the chair across from her.

"Look, I know it seems weird that she'd tell me anything about them or her past, but it just came up one day. It was minimal. There wasn't much information. I'm not holding out on you, honestly. I don't know much. All I know is that your mom will tell you more about her life and childhood when she's ready."

"It's been almost sixteen years and I barely know anything about her parents, but then, I was washing dishes last night and I noticed a pile of notes on the counter with this." She pulled out a sealed envelope, Roger and Virginia Tate scrolled across the recipient position and an address. "They're in Hot Springs, aren't they?"

Theo rubbed a hand over the back of his neck and hopped to his feet when his gaze lifted over her shoulder to see an approaching Reesa. "Got it!" Breathless, she plopped the dvd case on Clare's chair. "What are you two talking about?"

"Nothing." Clare's upbeat tone and hard stare at Theo had Reesa lifting a curious brow. "Really. Theo was just educating me on how to season vegetables."

"Oh." Reesa perked up at that news. "Yes, teach her your ways so she can cook for me." She released a shrill and evil cackle and Clare rolled her eyes as she secretively tucked the envelope back inside her pocket. "What can I do to help?"

Theo nodded to the chair next to Clare. "Have a seat. I've got it."

"Wow." Reesa beamed. "The royal treatment. You continue to surprise me, Theo."

He harumphed as he walked back inside the house to grab something, and Reesa turned on her daughter. "So, what did you guys talk about?"

"Nothing, really. He's not much of a talker, as you know, Mom."

"True. But he talks more to you than to me half the time."

Clare scoffed. "Yeah, right." The smidgen of bitterness in her tone had Reesa's eyes narrowing upon her daughter before Clare hopped to her feet and walked towards a basking Trooper as he laid stretched out on the deck. She rubbed a hand down his side and the dog instantly perked up, happy to play. "I'm going to play fetch with him for a bit." She walked off the porch, grabbing a well-loved tennis ball off one of the chairs, and Trooper scrambled to his feet in excitement.

Theo walked out as Clare threw the ball and he set a tray of steaks next to the grill. Reesa walked over, arms crossed over her chest as she scowled at him. He briefly glanced up and then back to his grill and then back at her. "What? What's that look for?"

"What did you say to her?"

"What?"

Reesa waved a hand to her aloof daughter. "She's mad about something. What did you say?"

"I didn't say anything."

"Clearly, you did. Clare doesn't act this way."

Theo rested his hands on his hips and peered down at her. "I didn't say anything to her, Reesa. We talked and she asked me a question that I did not answer."

"What question was that?"

Theo rubbed an anxious hand over the back of his neck. "You see, this is why I don't hang out with people. Drama. I don't want to be involved in anyone's mess."

"What drama? Clare and I don't have drama. We never have."

"Well, then whatever this is, I don't want to be in the middle of it. It's between you two. If you want to know what's wrong with her, ask her. Not me. I didn't cause her mood shift. You did. I'm just trying to mind my own business."

"Wait, I caused her teenage rudeness? How?"

Theo's exasperated expression had her nodding. "Oh, right. I'll handle this." She hurried towards her daughter and then slowed her pace, approaching Clare as she petted Trooper and wedged the tennis ball out of his mouth.

"I thought Theo had upset you."

"No. He's fine." Clare tossed the ball again and Trooper sailed through the yard after it.

"Then what is going on? You're moody."

"I'm almost sixteen. It's my right."

"But not while we are at someone's house, especially someone who is going out of his way to make us an amazing supper. We don't want to make Theo feel any more awkward than he already is."

Clare smirked at that, and her eyes flashed towards the deck. Theo continued working on their food, his eyes darting towards them periodically to check on them both. "I like him." Clare admitted. "And I think he likes you. Though he won't admit it, and he's not sure if he even wants to."

"We are not talking about Theo right now. Or me." Reesa waved a finger in Clare's face. "Don't change the subject. Tell me what *your* problem is."

Sighing, Clare reached into her back pocket and removed the envelope, handing it to Reesa. Reesa's heart sank. "Oh."

"Oh? Want to explain that to me?"

"Not really."

"This is why we moved to Piney, isn't it?"

Reesa ran a hand through her hair and reached for her daughter's hand. "Potentially. I haven't reached out to them yet, but was thinking about it."

"Why?"

"Because you're getting older, and I thought maybe they'd like to meet you... or something. I don't know." Reesa wriggled her fingers by her temple. "It made more sense up here."

"And if they don't want to meet me?"

"That's why I wrote a letter," Reesa explained. "I would leave it up to them to get in touch with me. If they did, okay. If they didn't, okay. We'd be fine. We've been fine. I just was trying to... extend an olive branch."

"As in me. I'm the olive branch."

"Kind of. You're everything to me. I think you've grown up to be an amazing person, and I started to feel bad that I'd kept them from knowing you all this time."

"They could have looked you up many times. It's not like you live off the grid, Mom."

"I was trying to be the bigger person, I guess. Forgive me for not filling you in just yet?"

"This once, I guess." Clare never held a grudge, one of the many attributes Reesa loved about her daughter.

"And don't be hard on Theo. I sort of blabbed out my life story the other day, and he just happened to be the victim forced to listen. He doesn't know much."

"That's sort of what he said too." Clare motioned towards him. "Should I go make it weird?"

Reesa's brow furrowed as she tried to figure out what Clare was thinking, and her daughter giggled as she ran up the deck stairs and threw her arms around an unsuspecting Theo. Theo stiffened immediately as Clare pressed her cheek into the middle of his back. Reesa bit back a laugh as she smiled at Theo's bewildered face at being dragged back into whatever was happening. Clare finally released him and then gave him an encouraging pat on the shoulder before running back towards Trooper.

Reesa giggled as she watched him place steaks on the grill. "She wanted to make it weird."

He just shook his head and rolled his eyes. "The apple doesn't fall far from the tree."

"Thanks for respecting my choice not to tell her yet. You could have explained everything I'd told you the other day, but you didn't. Thank you for letting me be the one to do that."

"It's your story, your plan, your choice. Don't see how it was my right to be the one to tell her."

"Even when she looked at you with those big puppy eyes?" Reesa asked.

"Well, she's got that mastered, that's for sure." Theo flipped a steak and closed the grill, turning to face her. "Glad you told her. She deserved to know."

"Yeah..." Reesa stepped towards him and lightly ran her fingers down his smooth cheek. "I'm getting used to this."

He swatted her hand away. "Well, don't. The beard is coming back."

"Ew, why?"

"Ew?" Offended, Theo balked at her reaction.

"Well, not *ew* ew... just ew. No. You can't. Look at your face, Theo. You can't tell me it doesn't feel better being free."

"Free?"

"Yes!" Reesa reached to cup his face and he took a step out of her reach. "Free."

"It feels weird," he argued.

"Then grow some stubble, but please do not go back to that bushman Duck Dynasty beard."

"What does it matter to you?" He reached for the bag of veggies as she determined to make things weird too. She reached for his free hand, and he turned in surprise as she pulled him towards her and wrapped her arms around his waist in a tight bear hug, her head snuggled right in the middle of his chest, a fitting spot for her. Theo froze, one hand hovering to his side, the other holding the bag of veggies. "What are you doing? Why are you hugging me? Why do you two make things so weird?"

Reesa chuckled against him as she tilted her head to look up at him. "It's what we do. I promise it will grow on you."

"Do I have a choice in that at all?"

"Always." Reesa beamed. She jumped to her tiptoes and planted a kiss on his cheek before stepping away from him. "You're a good man, Theo Whitley. Don't hide yourself away, especially behind a scruffy beard."

"I liked my beard," he mumbled under his breath.

"And don't sulk. You're too pretty to scowl now." Reesa winked at him as his cheeks flushed at being called pretty and he went back to checking the steaks.

"Are you ready to eat?"

"Yes. Starving."

"Good. Plates are on the counter in the kitchen if you want to grab them. These veggies are almost finished. Steaks are done." Reesa gave him a small pat on the back in thanks before walking into his house. She glanced around, the cabin style home similar in feel to the one she and Clare occupied, only bigger and sporting newer remodels. He was tidy, which wasn't a big surprise to her, really. He had simple furnishings, no fluff, not much color, though she could see some sentimentality in the throw blanket made up of old t-shirts from his high school years that was most definitely a gift from someone. She noticed a few framed photos on his fireplace hearth and walked over to see a younger version of Billy Lou and a man who must have been her late husband standing on either side of a young Theo, proudly embracing him as he wore a graduation cap. There was another photo of them together dressed in their Sunday best, their happiness warming her heart as she saw the love in all their faces at being with one another. It must have hit Theo hard when he lost his grandfather, she thought. It was obvious he and Billy Lou were close, but from the remaining photos, she could see a special bond between grandfather and grandson as well. The sliding glass door opened, and Theo walked in with a tray. "You get lost?"

"Sorry. I was looking at your photos." She pointed. "This is what I want for Clare." She pointed at the bond between him and his grandparents. "But it seems like an impossibility."

"You never know, it might happen." Theo shrugged his shoulders and began placing food on plates.

"I don't know." Uncertainty had her wrapping her arms around her middle as she walked towards his kitchen. "There was so much said back then, you know?"

He glanced up as he fished in his utensil drawer and withdrew silverware. "Have you forgiven them?"

"Yes." She shook her head. "And no. I don't know. I think I have, because I'd like to think I'm more mature than to hold a grudge for so long, but they completely abandoned me when I needed them most. I know I disappointed them, but I was their daughter. How could they do that? And then part of me is over it and just thankful I went through with it all because Clare is amazing, and my life has been great despite the hardships. So, it seems petty to still be upset with them. But when I think about introducing her to them, I flash back to that day of them just leaving me at the door of this sterile place and never coming back."

Theo exhaled a heavy breath and shook his head in disbelief. "I can't imagine doing that to anyone, much less my kid. And I can't imagine how it must have felt. I'm sorry you had to face that alone."

Reesa's eyes glassed over as she shrugged, and Theo gave an annoyed sigh as he set the utensils down and waved her towards him. Her lips twitched into a small smile as she bit back a quiet sob and stepped into his willing embrace. His strong arms wrapped around her and gently held her. It was all she needed and wanted. "You're getting good at this hugging thing."

He grunted and pulled her slightly away to look down at her. "You good?"

"If I say no, can I have another hug?"

He rolled his eyes, gave her one last big squeeze, and then released her.

"Thanks for being my friend, Theo, and dealing with my emotional rollercoaster as of late. I'm normally not this vulnerable around new people."

"Don't mention it. Though I'm going to kick you out of my house here soon if you don't let me eat this food."

"Got it." She darted to the door and yelled for Clare, the hungry teen rushing inside, out of breath, and his tired dog hot on her heels. "We have to eat now, or Theo's pop culture education will be cancelled for tonight."

Clare smiled at him, and Theo's lips tilted into a small smirk and his eyes twinkled. He didn't say much. He wasn't easy to pull information out of. He tried to act distant, but deep down, Reesa knew and could see that Theo Whitley liked having her and Clare around. He reached for both of their hands, the two of them surprised at his gesture, before he bowed his head and said a quick prayer over their meal.

"The night was a grand success." Jamie continued boasting about her evening out with Billy Lou. "The fundraiser brought in over $500,000 and Billy Lou said that was record-breaking for the organization."

"That's great." Theo listened as his friend chatted away about her evening, his eyes periodically darting towards the front windows whenever someone walked by on the sidewalk outside.

"And then I met the most amazing man. In fact, I think I'm going to marry him," Jamie continued.

"That's great, Jamie." Theo's voice trailed off as he blinked. "Wait, what?"

"Ah, so you *were* listening." Jamie chuckled. "I wasn't sure."

"I'm sorry." Theo rubbed a hand over the back of his neck in exasperation. "I'm a bit on edge this morning."

"I can tell. What's going on?"

"No. It's not about me. I want to hear about your night with Billy Lou. And I am listening this time."

"Nope. I want to know what's bouncin' around up there." She pointed to Theo's head. "You've been distracted since you came in this morning, and I know it's not from caffeine because I gave you decaf."

Theo glanced disgustingly at his cup. "Now, that's just mean."

Giggling, Jamie nodded. "Yep, so spill."

"I don't have anything to say. Last night Clare and Reesa hung out at my place, and it was…. new."

"Oh really?" Jamie cozied herself by leaning her elbows on her counter to listen more intently and to study her friend's face.

"Yeah. She brought Clare over so she could see my face." He rolled his eyes at that and at Jamie's bouncing eyebrows as she fanned herself in glee. "And I asked them to stay for supper."

"Wow." Jamie's same brows shot into her carrot-topped hairline. "That *is* new."

"Yeah." Theo looked as confused as she did. "And then we watched a movie. Well, Reesa and I did. Clare fell asleep about five minutes in."

"Double wow." Jamie attempted to hide her excitement by straightening and fidgeting with items on her counter. "Did you put your arm around her?" Jamie asked, her words excitedly lilting into a small squeal at the end.

Theo sighed and looked heavenward. "No, I was across the room."

"You didn't even sit by her?"

"No. She sat on the floor leaning against one of the chairs. Clare was in the chair, and I was on the couch."

"What did Clare think of it all?"

"She enjoyed it, I think. Seemed to, anyway." Theo shrugged.

"Daughter seal of approval. Impressive."

"I don't know about that." Theo shook his head as if to clear away the absurdity of Jamie's notions. "Anyway, it was a good time."

"But?"

"But what?"

"Your tone holds a but, T.J." Jamie pointed at him as she began making him a regular coffee to take with him to work.

"But I don't know, I don't do this sort of thing."

Jamie smiled. "So, you're interested in Reesa, and you're weirded out that you are?"

"No," Theo clarified. "I just don't understand how she gets me to do this kind of stuff. I mean, I hugged her. Willingly."

Jamie laughed. "Oh, T.J. You big softy."

"Yeah, well, it's sitting weird, that's all. And I just needed to bounce it off my best friend."

Her eyes danced and she held a hand to her heart for being called his best friend and he groaned. "Don't cry."

She giggled and flitted her hand towel at him. "I'm not. Okay, so you're interested in Reesa, but you don't know if you want to be or should be, and you're wondering when you'll see her again because you want to, but you're kind of weirded out that you want to, and you aren't sure if it's the direction you want to go."

Impressed, Theo's eyes widened slightly at her recap. "She's only been here a week. What do I know, right?"

"Time means nothing when it comes to this sort of stuff. The heart plays on a totally different playing field than the brain, so time is not a factor to consider."

"Spoken like a true romantic."

Jamie raised her hand. "Guilty." She beamed as she slid the cup of coffee his direction and her smile disappeared.

"What?" Theo asked, following her eyes out the front window and spotting Reesa on the sidewalk. He watched as a man he didn't recognize opened the door for her with a charming smile and Reesa stepped inside. Her eyes lit up at the sight of the two of them. "Good morning!"

"Hey." Jamie nodded over Reesa's shoulder to the man slowly approaching. "Who's your friend?"

"Oh. This is Rick." She waved towards Theo. "That's the man I was telling you about."

Rick stepped forward and extended a hand towards Theo. "Reesa tells me you're the owner of the mechanic garage here in town."

"I am."

Relief washed over the man's face. "Good, because I just left my car parked in front of it. I desperately need your help. Not sure what's going on with it, but it started smoking while in town, and I've got to be on the road."

Theo, not one to be rushed, stirred some cream into his milk.

"Reesa saw me stranded and offered to grab me a cup of coffee while we waited for your shop to open. What time do you open?"

"Nine."

"Those must be nice hours." Rick's annoyance at having to wait another half hour was obvious, but

Theo didn't quite care. It was Saturday and he opened an hour later on Saturdays.

"Just enough time for a coffee." Reesa pointed to Jamie. "This is Jamie. She makes the most amazing and bewitching concoctions."

"At your service." Jamie grinned, casting another eye at Theo as he watched Reesa interact with the man next to her. Jamie cleared her throat and Theo blinked, realizing he just stood to the side and hovered. He gave her a small nod of thanks as he began to walk off. Reesa left Rick at the counter and hurried after him.

"Theo." She grabbed his arm and he turned to face her. "Hey."

"Hey," he replied, waiting for her to continue.

"I was going to swing by your garage this morning."

"What for? Your car acting up?"

"No. No, it's great. Stellar job, by the way. Don't think I ever really thanked you for that." Reesa tucked a strand of her hair behind her ear as she flitted a nervous glance towards the counter. "I just wanted to say thanks for last night. Clare had a blast."

"And where is Clare this morning?" Theo glanced outside, and Reesa smiled that he was actually looking to visit with her daughter.

"She's still sleeping. Saturday mornings are sort of her days to bask in teenage life and take advantage of not waking up for school."

"Ah. Those were the days." He held up his coffee. "I need to go so I can get started on his car." He nodded towards Rick, and she smiled.

"Yeah. Hope you don't mind that I recommended you."

"Not at all."

Rick walked towards them, and Reesa welcomed him with a smile. "Theo is headed over to the garage now. Did you want to follow?"

Rick studied her a moment, his eyes traveling over her friendly demeanor, pretty face, and even a full swoop over her entire body, which Theo *did not* appreciate, before the man shook his head. "I left my number on the windshield. I figure Mr. T.J.," he nodded at Theo's shirt and name stitched on the front. "can let me know his thoughts once he's looked at it. Besides, it's not every day I'm stranded in the middle of nowhere with a beautiful woman as my guide."

Reesa's cheeks flushed as she gave Theo an amused look. Rick waved a hand towards one of the cozy corners. "Shall we?"

"Sure." Reesa patted Theo's arm in thanks as she led the way to the free chairs. She gave one last wave to Theo as he stood staring at them. He jolted to attention and walked out the door, irritation filling him as he fought off the urge to immediately dislike Rick. He wasn't paying attention when he ran smack dab into his grandmother.

"Theodore James," she scolded, jostling her purse. "You come barreling out that door like a bull after a flag and 'bout run me over."

He stabilized his grandmother by gently gripping her elbow. "Sorry, Grandma."

"I should say so. What has you in such a fit?"

"No fit, just focused on today's work." Theo pointed up the road to his garage. "Gotta go." He stormed off down the sidewalk, Billy Lou watching him leave. When she stepped inside the coffee shop and saw Reesa sitting with a handsome stranger, she immediately knew why her grandson was in such a mood.

CHAPTER EIGHT

Reesa accepted her second cup of coffee from Jamie and smiled up at her friend as Rick spoke into his cell phone to Theo about his car. "Am I looking at a few hours? Or a day? I'll pay double if you can fit me in this morning."

Reesa took a sip of her drink and wondered how frustrated that last comment must have made Theo. Theo didn't seem like a man that could be bought. If someone else's car was ahead of Rick's, that's how it would remain. She wasn't sure how Rick would handle that news.

"I understand. Thank you, T.J." Rick hung up. "Good man. Apparently, I have a faulty fuel injector. He recommends I replace them all."

"And are you?"

"Yes. He said it would take a few hours, but he would have me on the road by this afternoon." Rick beamed at his obvious triumph. "Which is great. I have to be in Hot Springs by three."

"I'm glad he was able to help you out. Theo's great."

"And are you two dating?" Rick asked.

Reesa flushed. "Oh, no, we aren't. He's actually my neighbor."

"Ah. I sensed familiarity between the two of you," Rick acknowledged. "But that's good news for me. I'm in need of a lunch date if I'm to be in this town for a few more hours. Would you mind?"

"Oh, well—" Reesa eyed an interested Jamie leaning her ear towards their conversation. "I would need to check with my daughter."

"Oh, you have a daughter?" Rick asked curiously.

Reesa nodded as she reached for her cell phone and dialed the cabin's phone number. Clare answered on the second ring, surprisingly chipper and awake. "Wow." Reesa smiled. "I wasn't expecting you to be so alert."

"Hey, Mom." Clare muffled around a bite in her mouth. "Hey, is it okay if I venture into town with Teddy? He offered to come pick me up and we were going to grab coffee at Jamie's with a few other friends."

"That's fine. I'm actually here now."

"Oh, great, because my second question was if I could borrow some cash." Clare laughed into the phone.

"Of course it was. Just remember, 'Five dollars each. Five dollars is all my mom allows me to spend.'"

"Mom, I'm not sure that's an appropriate quote," Clare laughed.

"What? It's Full Metal Jacket!" Reesa challenged.

"Um, yeah, but it's also the quote that comes from negotiating with a prostitute."

"Is it?" Reesa looked confused and thought a moment. "Oops."

"Yeah," Clare laughed. "We'll be there in a bit. Thanks, Mom."

Reesa hung up. "She's actually headed into town with some friends, so I guess I'm good. Though I have to be here to hand over some money. Typical teenager; she doesn't have any cash on her."

"How old is she?" Rick asked.

"Fifteen." Reesa could see the realization hit him, but he was too polite to say anything. She could also tell the news didn't sit well with him. She was used to the response. He'd be polite a bit longer, but the idea of a woman with a teenage kid seemed to weird men out a lot of times. She now just waited for his excuse to leave. It would come. She could already tell. Instead of being annoyed, hurt, or discouraged, Reesa began laying the groundwork to make it an easier task for him. "You know, I would love to do lunch today, but I just remembered that I promised my friend Billy Lou I would help her sort through some old boxes of stuff at her house." It wasn't true. Yet. Reesa imagined she could call up Billy Lou and offer just that and the woman would find boxes from somewhere. She'd buzzed into the shop earlier for her coffee and would no doubt still be in town and at the salon chatting.

"Ah, well, that's no problem." Rick quickly bounced back to his charming demeanor. "Perhaps another time."

She knew there would be no other time. She also knew he would avoid Piney at all costs after his car was fixed. Rick was the type of man that passed through and promised to call and then never did. He was easy to spot. And if she were the kind of woman up for short flings of passion or a random stranger make-out session, she'd fall right into his trap of charm. But she wasn't that kind of woman. And at this point in her life, she wasn't sure she wanted romance at all. She wanted to enjoy her last few years with Clare at home and then maybe she could focus more on herself. When Clare walked in with her new friends, Reesa welcomed the interruption and used it as her excuse to head out so as not to crimp her daughter's style by lingering amongst her friends. Rick didn't seem too disappointed and was friendly enough to give her a kind farewell wave before opening his laptop.

"Who is that?" Clare nodded over Reesa's shoulder as Reesa fished in her wallet for cash.

"A man passing through. Hi, Teddy," Reesa greeted.

Teddy smiled. "Ms. Tate."

She smirked at his manners; being called 'Ms. Tate' always made her feel slightly like a schoolmarm. She handed Clare a twenty-dollar bill. "Just in case you guys go to lunch."

"Thanks." Clare gave her a tight hug. "I think we are going to swim at Teddy's house after this and his mom was going to order pizzas for us. It okay if I hang with him for the day?"

"Of course." Reesa nodded. "I'm going to go discuss some things with Theo and then might hang out with Billy Lou."

"Discuss, as in you're going to go bug Theo before meeting up with Billy Lou?" Clare prodded.

"Exactly." Reesa beamed.

Chuckling, Teddy nodded towards the coffee counter. "I'm going to order. Want me to order for you, Clare?"

"Sure. Caramel frapp, please."

"You got it." He gave a small wave towards Reesa as he trudged up to the counter with their other friends.

"I think I like that kid," Reesa admitted. "He's growing on me."

"He's pretty cool," Clare agreed. "You okay? You seem sort of... down."

"Me?" Reesa asked.

"Yeah. Did that guy hurt your feelings or something?"

"What?" Reesa's brows lifted slightly in surprise that Clare could pick up on her disappointment in Rick. "No. He's fine. Just a friendly stranger passing through. Theo is working on his car."

Clare squeezed her hand. "You're cool that I'm hanging out with friends? I know this is our first real weekend to just chill together in our new place."

"Of course I'm cool," Reesa assured her. "You have fun with your new friends. I'm an independent woman. I can entertain myself." She winked.

"Okay." Clare perked up and gave her one last big squeeze before stepping up next to her lanky friend. Jamie gave her an encouraging nod and Reesa knew Clare was watched after regardless of whether she was present or not. The joys of a small town, and Reesa loved it more and more.

She stepped out onto the curb and walked towards Theo's garage, her mind wandering to the current pattern she was creating. She'd need to draft it soon. Her notes had started to overwhelm her, which meant it was time to transfer them to computer and sort them and get them ready for publication. She hoped to release the pattern by the end of the month. She opened the door to

Theo's office and found a rusty stool next to his desk and sat. If she could turn the double crochet on the third round into a treble stitch, she could lengthen that row and have more of a pop of color. That could work. She loved the blue she'd chosen, an aquamarine. She would just have to unravel two rows to go back and correct. She could do that though, for the sake of the pattern. A throat cleared and she snapped out of her daze and noticed Theo sitting at his desk staring at her.

"Reesa," he greeted.

"Hey." She tucked her hair behind her ears. "What's up?"

Theo's eyes narrowed as he studied her. "Oh, just working... at my desk... in my office... where you just walked in for no reason. You?"

"I thought I would come and—" She hadn't really thought that far ahead. She'd just needed some air and a place to go after departing from Rick. "Wait for Billy Lou."

"She's at the salon." Theo pointed across the street.

"I know."

"So why not wait there?"

"Maybe I find your company better than a lot of old ladies," Reesa challenged.

"You'd be the first." He tossed his pencil onto his desk and leaned back in his chair to stare up at her, his arms crossing over his broad chest. "What's really going on? I thought you were being wined and dined today by the city guy." He nodded to the sporty car parked inside his garage.

"Not quite. Hey, do you mind if I sit in here for a bit? I promise I won't get in your way or stop you from working." She held up two fingers in a scout's honor salute.

Theo leaned forward. "Did something happen?" His voice dropped so as not to be overheard and she gently reached a hand towards him and rested it on his upper arm. The muscle beneath made her smile as she gave it a quick squeeze and had Theo rolling his eyes and pulling back, all sympathy leaving his expression. "Okay, for a few minutes. But then you have to leave. I have work to do."

"Am I distracting you?" Reesa wriggled her eyebrows.

"No." Theo nodded towards the window overlooking his garage without even glancing up from his computer. "You're distracting them."

Reesa peered out the window and saw Mike and two other men eyeing them in the office. She offered a friendly wave and then looked at Theo. "Have you ever thought about having a carwash attached to your shop?"

"No." He didn't look up as he typed some numbers on his keyboard and the printer next to his desk began to shoot out a piece of paper.

"Have you noticed there is no carwash in town?"

"There is on the way to Hot Springs."

"On the way, yes, but not here in Piney."

"So just cross the Ouachita River and go to the closest one... on the way to Hot Springs."

"You're missing the point, Theo."

"I wish you'd get there, then."

"I'm saying, if you added on a little automatic carwash next to your garage, it would do well here. Diversify your income, as they say."

"Who says?" Theo asked.

"Business gurus." He grunted so she continued. "I mean, I'd use it."

"People have water hoses and have washed their vehicles at home for years. I don't think a new fancy carwash is going to change their mind."

"Yeah, but who likes doing that? Nobody. I need to wash my car right now, but I have no desire to do it outside. I'd rather zip into a carwash, wait a few minutes, and come out sparkly clean."

Theo sighed and turned to face her. "Reesa, you need to go."

His words stung and his stern face relaxed into a small smirk, one she'd come to like seeing now that she could. And though he'd grown a small shadow of stubble over his face, the beard had yet to return and she liked seeing his full expressions. "I can't get work done with you here."

"Well, stop talking to me then."

"That's a bit hard to do since you keep talking to me."

"I'll stop."

"No, you need to go. I thought you were waiting on Billy Lou anyway."

"Yeah, that was my excuse. I haven't even talked to her yet."

"She would welcome you with open arms, and she has more time today than I do. Especially if I'm going to have that Rick guy on the road by three."

"Please do," Reesa mumbled. "Alright." She hopped off the stool. "I'll leave." She stretched a moment. "I'll bug Billy Lou and then procrastinate from my own work further by washing my car... with a water hose... like a caveman."

Theo stood and opened the office door for her. She paused in front of him and looked up at him, his hand gripping the edge of the glass door to keep it ajar. "Will you eat supper with us tonight?" She could tell her question surprised him. It surprised her too. But Theo's presence was like a soothing balm to her crazy morning, and she wasn't quite ready to let that go.

"What time?" he asked, and her face lifted into a beaming smile.

"Whenever you get home and showered, just head on over." She leaned up on the very tips of her toes and kissed his cheek, stumbling from the over-extension to do so and catching herself against his chest. His free hand lightly touched her hip to help stabilize her. "Thanks. See you then." She lightly patted his chest with the hand that had rested there and walked out.

~

"Did you let Reesa know I would be joining you?" Billy Lou asked. "I'd hate to turn up unannounced."

"It's fine," Theo assured her.

"Well, it was sweet of her to ask us over." Billy Lou eyed her grandson from the corner of her eye. "Betty said she saw Reesa at the garage this mornin'. Said she saw you two kiss."

Theo's foot tapped the break with a little too much force as he began to turn onto his driveway from the highway. Billy Lou bit back a smile at his reaction. "We did not kiss."

"Well, she seemed adamant that you had."

"She was mistaken."

"Oh. Well, I'll be sure to set the record straight," Billy Lou affirmed. "Betty's good at spreading rumors."

He parked his truck out front of his house. "I'll just be a few minutes. If you wouldn't mind, could you pick some tomatoes to take over? Clare can't get enough of them."

Billy Lou watched him hurry inside and bit back a smile as she did what he asked. He walked back out less than ten minutes later, clean and changed into fresh clothes. "Ready?" he asked.

"Of course." She eyed the beer in his hand. "You didn't grab one for your granny?"

He flushed and handed her the one he had and hurried inside to grab another for himself. "Alright, now are you ready?"

She handed him four tomatoes and he whistled for Trooper to hop in the back of the truck. When they pulled in front of Reesa's cabin, her rear end stuck out of the back passenger door in short cut off shorts. She was barefoot and a long extension hose from a shop vacuum wove into her car, the sound of it loud against the quiet woods. Clare hopped off the front porch steps at their arrival and she walked towards his truck in greeting, her eyes lighting up at Trooper and the tomatoes Theo'd brought her. She hugged Billy Lou and waved a 'pay her no mind' hand in her mom's direction. She ushered them inside, the smell of food permeating the colorful interior. "Mom's been cleaning her car the last several hours. She should be almost done."

"Good to see you, sweetie." Billy Lou ran a tender hand down Clare's long ponytail. "How's school?"

"Great. I actually really like it. I've made some friends, thanks to Teddy. Even had coffee with a few of them this morning."

"That's wonderful." Billy Lou beamed.

Reesa walked inside, her face flushed and sweat glistening along her neck and collarbone as the oversized t-shirt slid to the side and ran off the shoulder. "Hey," she greeted on a heavy exhale.

"Hey, yourself." Billy Lou noted how her grandson's eyes lingered on the pretty woman across the room, but he didn't say anything. Instead, his wary expression shifted back to Clare.

"Aren't you worn out?" Billy Lou clucked. "My goodness, workin' hard out there."

"I know. I've been out there for three hours washing and cleaning out my car." Her eyes narrowed on Theo. "Sure would be nice if someone had a carwash around here. I could have been done in half the time."

Theo grunted. "But don't you feel good about all your hard work?" His sarcastic tone had her grinning.

"Oh yes. I even used all the little attachments on the vacuum cleaner. Except that little round one. What is that one for anyway?"

"Nobody knows," Billy Lou confirmed on a laugh.

"Well, I didn't anticipate it taking me *this* long, but I'm going to grab a quick shower and then supper should be ready." She looked to Clare and her daughter nodded as she glanced at a timer that sat on the counter.

"Take your time, honey. And thank you for inviting us."

Reesa flashed a curious glance at Theo at his grandmother's comment, but he nervously avoided her gaze. "Of course." Reesa smiled. "Be back in a few."

She'd barely made it down the hallway when Theo excused himself from the table and followed after her. Billy Lou and Clare exchanged amused expressions before beginning their own conversation about Clare's classes and new friends. Theo caught up with Reesa at her bedroom door, the scent of her pouring out of the open doorway and slamming him right in the gut. His stomach clenched as she turned to him in surprise. "Did you need something?"

Theo didn't really know what he'd planned to say. He hadn't meant to follow her all the way to her room. He'd meant to just catch her and say, 'Hey, sorry I brought my grandmother because I'm a coward and didn't know how to handle what I've started to feel when I'm around you.' But he didn't say that. He couldn't say that. He wasn't ready to say something like that. He just wasn't prepared to see her walk off in the cute shorts and sloppy shirt. Her beautiful shoulder peeking out, the curve of her neck, the exposed toes with purple nail polish beckoned him like a returning soldier to his lost love. He just wanted to stare at her and soak in the image of her.

"Theo?" Reesa reached out to give him a light shake, and he jolted at her touch as though she'd electrocuted him. "Whoa." She acknowledged he was on edge, but her eyes showed she had no clue as to why, thankfully. He had time to recover from his lapse of mental awareness.

"I, uh, just wanted to say that I'm sorry I brought Billy Lou unannounced. She was with me..." He paused, not liking the lie that began to form on his lips. "You know what, that's a lie. She wasn't with me. I invited her."

"That's fine. She's always welcome here. We love the both of you." She smiled and nodded over her shoulder. "I'm going to get showered. I'll be out in a few minutes."

Theo lingered a moment longer, his fingers betraying him as they reached out and gently trailed down the silky curve of her neck he'd been eyeing since he drove up. He ended their dance by lightly twisting them in the edges of her hair that rested on her shoulder. It was as soft as he'd imagined, and he gave it a playful tug before releasing it. He cleared his throat, not knowing what to say and completely flummoxed as to why he'd just done what he did. Reesa's eyes bored into him as he turned to walk away. He felt them piercing his back until he rounded the wall and emerged back in the kitchen. He heard her bedroom door close and breathed a bit easier at the barrier that was now between them. What was he doing? What was he thinking?

"Everything alright?" Billy Lou asked.

"Fine." Theo took a sip of his beer as Clare hopped out of her seat at the sound of the timer and pulled a dish out of the oven. She set it on top of the stove and then lifted a lid of a saucepan and stirred its contents. "Smells good," he complimented.

She blushed. "Well, I'm hoping it is. Mom and I have been experimenting in the kitchen lately. We're not the most awesome of cooks, but we're learning... I think. Tonight is supposed to be an Italian pasta bake and we made green beans from the ones you gave us from your garden. I hope I did it right. They seem soft." Uncertainty had her poking at the beans in the pan.

"I'm sure it is all delicious." Billy Lou beamed proudly. "I love that you two are trying something new. It's never too late to learn."

"Mom has sort of started panicking the last year or so, ever since I started high school. She thinks she's completely failed as a mother by not teaching me basic things, like cooking. She hasn't failed, but it seems like she's trying to teach me random things lately to prepare me for life or something."

"Oh, I remember being like that with Theo." Billy Lou laughed. "Remember me teaching you how to sew on a button?" She laughed as Clare's face brightened. "His big hands and fingers were so clumsy. He begged me to stop because he'd poked himself so many times with the needle. But we pulled through, didn't we?" She patted Theo's knee. "And now he can replace a button on his shirt if need be."

"I've only ever had to do it once," Theo acknowledged.

"Because I still do it." Billy Lou admitted on a whisper to Clare. "But I don't mind. Keeps me useful."

"What's useful?" Reesa's voice asked as she stepped into the kitchen.

"Sewing," Clare answered

"Oh, I thought you were talking about *how useful a carwash would be*," she stressed in loud tones right behind Theo. He acted completely unaware of her hint and nonchalantly took a sip of his beer. She playfully shoved his shoulder as she looked at Billy Lou. "I told him he should open one next to his garage."

"That would be wonderful." Billy Lou agreed. "Definitely something to consider, Theodore."

He grunted in acknowledgment and Reesa sighed. "That's all he does when I mention it. Grunt. It's like Theo language for 'Yeah, that's a no.'"

Billy Lou laughed. "Boy, does she have you pegged."

"Maybe I just like to grunt," Theo challenged, his eyes flashing up to hers. Her cheeks tinted a light shade of pink when he stared at her and something shifted between the two of them, an undercurrent that washed back and forth like subtle waves on the water. He felt it, and he could tell she did too. What it was, he didn't know, but it was there lingering beneath the surface of their every interaction. It'd been there since he met her, but it'd slowly expanded to the point of making a room quiet and slightly awkward.
Clare hopped to her feet again. "Supper?" she asked, easing the tension in the room.

"Love some!" Billy Lou chimed in, her overly chipper tone a warning to her grandson to get himself together.

Theo took the hint and accepted the plateful of food Clare slid in front of him. She'd put half the pan of food on his plate and his eyes widened. "Is it too much?"

Reesa turned and her eyes lit up as she laughed. "Oh my. Here." She grabbed his plate and put half on hers. "He's a big guy, Clare, but I don't think he's a bear."

"Well, I don't know how much guys eat. Teddy would eat this whole pan if you put it in front of him and he's a skinny dude. Theo is twice the size of him, so I just assumed he required a lot of food."

"Honey, you just fill it on up. Our boys need some sustenance every now and then," Billy Lou encouraged.

"Well, maybe as we experiment more, we can bring you food all the time." Clare smiled at Theo as he took a hearty bite of the pasta and gave her a thumbs up at the taste.

"I don't know if Theo would want some of our experiments," Reesa admitted. "We've missed the mark on a few of them."

"That's what pizza nights are for, sweetie." Billy Lou patted Reesa's thigh affectionately. "You should come by the house some time and we can cook together. I love to cook."

"Really?" Reesa asked. "I'd love to learn from you, Billy Lou."

"Well consider it a date, then. How about we have Monday and Wednesday meals at my house?" She looked to the two women and then Theo.

"Grandma, they have lives of their own. I doubt they'd—"

"I'd love to," Reesa interrupted. "Clare?"

"I'm down." The teenager grinned at Theo with a smug smile as if to say he had no escape.

"With or without you, Theodore, we will have some good food and good fellowship." Billy Lou squeezed Clare's hand in excitement at having future company. "And your friends are welcome anytime too, girlie."

"Awesome." Clare nodded enthusiastically.

"Did you finish that handsome city slicker's car today, Theodore?" Billy Lou asked.

Theo nodded. "Yes. Thankfully. He was at the garage at one urging us to move faster."

Billy Lou shook her head in resignation. "Some people just don't know how to slow down and enjoy life these days. Piney isn't a town you just zoom through. You have to linger and mosey along to enjoy it best."

"I don't think he was here to enjoy the town, Grandma. Just passing through."

"Well, that's fine too. We only keep the best." She winked at Reesa as she took a bite of her meal.

"Billy Lou," Reesa hesitantly began. "I have a question for you, and I completely understand if you say no, and it will not hurt my feelings. It's completely off topic, so excuse me for changing the subject."

"Alright..."

"I was wondering if I could possibly build a small deck off the back porch of the cabin?" Reesa asked. "It has the perfect shade from the pines, and after hanging out at Theo's and enjoying his deck, I think it'd be nice to have one here for Clare and me. We love being outside."

"Oh, I think that's a wonderful idea!"

"I will cover the costs," Reesa went on. "I just didn't want to do it without asking first."

"Oh, pish posh, I will pay for it."

"No, no, no," Reesa continued. "I will. It was my idea and it's not a necessary expense."

"Honey, I have too much money to just sit on it, and this is my property. I will pay for it. I'm just thrilled someone wants to do something with this place. And you girls have just livened it up with all your color and beautiful things. I consider it a worthy investment."

"Well, thank you. I was hoping to drive into Hot Springs and look at lumber on Monday."

"I'll ride along. We can have the day, eat a fun lunch, and then come back to my place for supper." Billy Lou laid out the plan and Reesa readily agreed. "You will join us, Theodore."

"Can't go to Hot Springs."

"I meant for supper," Billy Lou corrected him, and he nodded his acquiescence, knowing it was pointless to argue with his grandmother. "This will be so much fun!" She clapped her hands together in giddy excitement.

Reesa chuckled and glanced at Theo, his frowning face causing her eyes to sober. "You don't have to join us for supper if you have plans." She gave him an out, and he wanted to take it. Not because he didn't want to spend time with Billy Lou, or her, or even Clare, but because he did. He wanted to. That was the problem. He *wanted* to. And he wasn't ready to want something like that. He'd never really wanted that with anyone before. He liked his life quiet, uninterrupted, and predictable. Reesa was opposite all of those things. She required attention. She deserved attention. And he just wasn't sure yet if he wanted to be the guy to give it to her. Was it wrong for him to question it? To question her? To question himself? He would admit he hadn't been drawn to anyone in years the way he was drawn to Reesa. She seemed completely at ease with how he was: his not-so-friendly manners, his quiet personality. But he'd just met her. There was still much he didn't know about her. And he couldn't make a decision just on attraction. And he'd admit he was definitely attracted to her. And that surprised him too because she came out of nowhere. And that left him feeling a bit unsettled. She just sort of popped into his life and now he was left to figure out how to fit her into it. He needed time to do that without her constantly being present. He wasn't sure if he'd have that sort of luck with Reesa; she seemed to be everywhere, even in his thoughts, even if she wasn't physically standing there.

"Theodore?" Billy Lou snapped in front of his face. His eyes, dazed and staring at Reesa, blinked into focus and he shook his head.

"Hm?"

"You alright? We lost you for a moment."

"Just thinking." He focused on the last bites of his meal and stood to clear his plate. "I need to head back to the house."

Disappointment covered his grandmother's face. "We'll take you home, Billy Lou," Reesa offered. "We'd love for you hang out longer."

"If it's not too much trouble, I'd like that too," Billy Lou admitted.

Reesa looked up at Theo as she stood to walk him to the door. "Thanks for coming over."

"Thanks for supper. My compliments to the chef." He tapped his temple in a salute towards Clare and she grinned proudly before turning her attention back to his grandmother. He stepped out on the porch and whistled, Trooper bounding through the tree line towards him, tongue lolling to the side as he panted. He felt Reesa's fingers weave through his as she squeezed his hand, the touch sending sporadic charges cycling up his arm. It was just a short squeeze of thanks, but the aftermath of her touch had his mind whirling.

"Listen, if we ever overstep or upset you in any way, please tell me, okay?" Her worried eyes landed on his and he nodded quietly.

"You're fine."

She forced a smile and shook her head. "I know that's a lie somehow, and I don't know if you're just too polite to bring it up or if you just don't want to tell me in general, but I don't want to do anything to upset you, Theo."

"You haven't."

Doubt lingered with concern on her face, and he rubbed a hand over the back of his neck. "Look, you're fine. You and Clare are fine. I just... have a lot on my mind right now."

"I'll pretend to believe you," she said quietly, her eyes leaving his to look out over the peaceful yard. "Was it because I came to your work today? I won't do that again." She looked at him for clarification.

"No, that was fine. You're fine, Reesa. It's nothing. I've just got to sort some stuff out. That's all."

"Is it Clare?" Her voice wavered a bit. "If you're uncomfortable with her hanging out with Billy Lou or—"

"Would you stop it?" His voice was sharp and loud, and she leaned back in surprise. "There is absolutely nothing wrong with Clare or you. Got it?"

She gave a nervous nod.

"I'm just cranky. I have lots on my mind, like I said. I'm not upset with you or with you being here. Got it?" His tone could slice through diamonds.

She nodded again, though her face told him she still wasn't convinced.

"Geez, Reesa." He combed his hands through his hair. "Go inside, okay. Enjoy your time with Billy Lou."

Her lip quivered and her eyes glassed over as if she were barely holding in her emotions at him raising his voice at her. He inhaled and exhaled to calm down. "Look," he gently reached for her hand, and she took a cautious step back, which made him cringe even more at his own behavior. "I didn't mean to yell at you." He finally reached her fingers and drew her towards him into an embrace. She slowly relaxed against him, and he breathed in the scent of her. "I'm just... not used to having someone around who actually wants to spend time with me. I need to get used to it is all."

"You don't have to if you don't want to." Her voice was muffled against him, and he hugged her tighter.

"I want to," he assured her. "I do." His voice quieted and his hand brushed down the back of her hair still damp from her shower. He heard her sniffle, and he tugged her back enough to see he'd made her cry. "Oh geez."

She sniffed back a laugh. "I'm fine. I cry about everything."

"Well, I don't want to make you cry, so you can stop doing it now."

She flashed a watery smile. "Now, I like to hear that. You're a good person, Theo. I needed to be reminded of that today when I came to your office."

"Did I do something to cause you to need reassurance in me?"

"No. Not you. Rick sort of just disappointed me a bit and reminded me of a lot of past situations and men. I needed a reminder that there were still good men out there, so I went to see the only one I know right now."

Her comment warmed him though part of him wanted to pummel the Rick guy at the same time. "And then I kicked you out of my office. I'm sorry for that."

"I knew you would," she chuckled. "But I didn't mind. Because you're still my friend and deep down, you're kind. Besides, you pretend to be annoyed by us, but I can tell you like us." She motioned towards Clare over her shoulder, and he nodded that he did like them. "And that means a lot. So, thanks. But the demand is still there that if we ever do anything to upset you or overwhelm you, please tell me."

"Yeah, well, right now is one of those moments then. Not upset, just overwhelmed." He motioned towards the cozy kitchen scene. "I'm not used to socializing much, so give me time to get used to it."

"Deal." She smiled and leaned her head against his heart once more. "I'm getting to where I really like these Vin Diesel hugs." He purposely removed her arms from around him and she laughed. "Bummer, I had to go and make it awkward, didn't I?"

"Just a word of advice." Theo began his walk back towards his truck and turned to offer his last tidbit. "Don't ever talk about another man when you're in my arms, alright?"

She placed her hands on her hips as she studied his serious face and she nodded. "I think I can do that, as long as you promise to hug me more." Her eyes twinkled at the curveball she knew she'd thrown at him.

He could play the game too and responded with a very serious and full-hearted reply of, "I think I can do that." Their eyes held a moment longer before he climbed in his truck and drove his way home.

CHAPTER NINE

"*Thank you for today,* Billy Lou." Reesa leaned her head against the leather headrest of Billy Lou's SUV and closed her eyes. "I feel productive and ambitious."

"I'm so glad!" Billy Lou smiled as she turned out of the parking lot of the hardware store and out onto the busy street. "That lumber won't be far behind us, so we better head back to the cabin. I'll drop you off there. I'll whip up some supper and bring it over later. That way you're at home when they deliver the supplies."

"Did we bite off more than we can chew?" Reesa asked.

"Absolutely not," Billy Lou assured her. "It's going to look fabulous. I live for projects, Reesa."

"Your sketches were beautiful. I hope I can make them come to fruition."

"You will. Take your time. Don't be afraid to ask Theo for help."

"No, I want to do this myself. I don't want to bother him any more than I already have. Besides, I want him to be surprised by the finished product."

Billy Lou's brightly painted lips tilted up at the corners. "Oh, I think he will be. How could he not? Now, is there anything else we need to do on the way out of town?"

"Actually, could you buzz by one of the post office boxes in front of that shopping center?" Reesa pointed to the right and Billy Lou turned into a parking lot and eased to a stop by the familiar blue drop box. Reesa fished in her purse and withdrew the letter to her parents, hesitating a moment as she read their names and address.

"It's never going to happen if you don't drop it in there," Billy Lou whispered, reaching across the center console and squeezing Reesa's free hand.

Reesa's throat tightened as her vision blurred. She sniffed back the tears that threatened to come. "It's a long story, Billy Lou."

"I didn't ask." Billy Lou pointed at the letter. "I'm making assumptions in my head about who that letter is meant for, but even without my assumptions I can see it's a difficult task for you. And I'm here for you whether you put it in that blue box or not."

Reesa held up the letter with both hands, studied it a moment longer, and then rolled down her window and slid it into the drop box before she could chicken out. "There. It's done. The ball is in their court now." She felt her hands begin to shake and she clasped them tightly together to stop the flood of emotions—the fear—before it could take over. "I did it," she whispered. "I actually did it."

Billy Lou patted her thigh. "You're a brave woman, Reesa. And a lovely one at that. Clare is a gem too. Should nothing come of that letter, I want you to know that you will always have me in your corner. Theo too. Should something wonderful happen because of that letter, I hope you'll still stick around Piney for a long time, because I'd hate to see you leave."

Reesa flashed a watery smile. "Thanks, Billy Lou." She pushed her hair out of her face and rubbed her hands over her face. "Okay, it's done. We can go now. We have a fun project to look forward to. My parents, should they want to get in touch, now have a way to do so."

"Ah." Billy Lou, finally realizing who the letter was intended for, gently patted Reesa's leg again before shifting into gear and heading towards home. "They'd be right fools to not want to see you girls. Fools."

Reesa grinned as she grabbed her cell phone out of her purse. "I'm going to text Theo. He's sort of known that the whole reason I moved to Piney was for this to potentially happen. I want him to know I finally mailed the letter. And should they want to meet, I have a feeling he will have to suffer the emotional disaster I will be leading up to it. Best prepare him now."

Chuckling, Billy Lou nodded for her to go ahead, and Reesa sent a short message of: "*I mailed it. The letter to my parents. I mailed it.*"

A few minutes later a simple, "*ok*", popped up on her screen, followed by, "*And how do you feel?*"

"*Terrified.*" At least she was being honest with him. She was terrified. Nervous. Heartbroken all over again. Flashes of every hardship she'd encountered where she remembered wishing for her parents' help or presence raced through her mind. Those were a long time ago, though. She didn't need her parents now. She'd raised Clare to the best of her abilities. She'd provided for her, and even if it took years of struggling, they'd made it together. And now, she had an amazing young woman on her hands that she didn't want to ever let go of, though she knew eventually that time would come. She still had a few years with Clare at home, thank goodness, but already she grieved the day her chapter of having Clare under her roof would be gone. She wouldn't just drop her off at college or wherever and leave either. She'd linger. Force herself into her daughter's life for visits and trips and random shopping sprees. She'd always be there for Clare. There would never be a day that went by that her daughter would feel unwanted, unloved, or abandoned. Ever. Her cell phone rang, and she nervously glanced at Billy Lou.

"Honey, they haven't gotten that letter yet. Best see who it is." She smiled tenderly as Reesa scrambled for her phone in the seat.

Relief washed over her as she answered. "Hey."

Theo's deep voice carried through the phone. "You alright?" His simple question as to her mental status was appreciated and touched her, as if he'd known she'd need more to calm her down than just a simple text.

"I'm okay, I think. Just nervous." Reesa fiddled with an unraveling string on her pant leg. "Trying not to turn into a blubbery, sobbing mess in Billy Lou's nice car."

"She wouldn't care," Theo assured her.

"I know, but I'd rather not. I already feel better hearing your voice. Thanks for calling me." Silence hung on the phone, and she hoped she hadn't scared him off with her last comment.

"Just wanted to make sure you were okay."

"Thanks. You're coming over for supper, right? Billy Lou is dropping me off at the house because we bought the wood needed to build the deck and they're delivering like, right behind us. But she's going to bring supper over to my place."

"I'll be there. I might be a bit late today. I'm still working on a couple of things here." She could hear the sounds of metal clanging and a tool being jostled amongst its comrades.

"Whenever is fine. We'll have to show you our plans."

"I imagine they are over the top considering my grandmother is helping you."

Reesa grinned into the phone. "Sort of. I think Billy Lou overestimates my building capabilities."

"Not true!" Billy Lou called out to be heard through the line.

"Jamie coming over too?" Theo asked.

"You know, I didn't ask her. But I will. That's a good idea. She'll be excited about the project too. And she'll want to know I mailed the letter. She's been after me to do so."

"She could probably bring Clare home too. I saw her and her friends walk to the coffee shop a while ago. They might still be there."

"Are you keeping tabs on my unruly teenager for me, Theo?"

"Just happened to look up."

"Right. Well, I appreciate it, nonetheless. I'll text Jamie and Clare and share the plan. And again, thanks for calling me. You've settled me a bit." A long, awkward silence. "Theo?"

"Yep. I'm here. I, um, will see you in a bit."

"In case I don't see ya, good afternoon, good evening, and goodnight."

Sighing, Theo replied, "Let me guess... that's from a movie?"

Laughing, Reesa leaned comfortably back in her seat. "You're starting to get me, Theodore Whitley."

"Yeah, well, I'm trying. I have no idea where it's from, I could just tell. See you later."

"Bye. The Truman Show. Okay, bye!" She hurried to add before hearing him hang up. She smiled at her phone as she quickly shot a text to Jamie and Clare, filling them in on the plans for the evening. "Theo will be a little late, but he's coming. I am inviting Jamie too, if that's alright?"

"Of course. The more the merrier." Billy Lou exited towards Piney and decreased her speed to accommodate the slight turn that pointed them away from town and towards the cabin. "You've been good for him, you know."

"Hm?" Reesa looked up from her phone and noticed Billy Lou quickly glance her direction and then back to the road. "For Theo. He's come out of his shell the last couple of weeks, and I know it is because of you. It makes me happy to see him interacting with people again."

"Well, I haven't really given him much of a choice." Reesa chuckled. "I'm pretty sure I tread his last nerve every time he's around me. But I can tell he likes us. He's kind to Clare, and I appreciate that more than anything."

"She's a lovely girl. Beautiful, smart, funny, and has your charm. You've done a wonderful job with her, honey. I'm sure it hasn't been easy being a single mother, but you two are peas in a pod, and she's happy. And that says a lot about your parenting right there. If your baby is happy, then you must be doing something right." Billy Lou nodded with gumption and flicked her blinker to turn.

"Thanks." Reesa sighed in relief as she saw the cabin come into view. The little run-down house already tugged at her heart and had become special to her. She noticed two new brightly colored flowerpots on the front steps and knew Clare must have found them somewhere and brought them home. The vivid flowers in them told her Billy Lou had filled them with cuttings from her own house. Slowly, they were turning the little house into their home, and deep in her heart Reesa could feel that comfortable pull that came from knowing you were finally home. She'd only ever had that feeling once when she was young, before life carried her in a different direction. But to feel that soothing peace fill her heart again confirmed even more that she was in the right spot at the right time and with the right people. Whether her parents answered her letter or not didn't matter. She and Clare had found a place to call home and Reesa envisioned the move to Piney being long-term regardless of her parents. When Billy Lou shifted into park outside the cabin, Reesa shouldered her purse. "Thank you again, Billy Lou. I had fun today."

"Oh, me too, honey." She smiled. "I'll be back here in a bit with a warm supper. You just have some tea made."

"Will do." Reesa slid out of the SUV and waved as Billy Lou hightailed it down the bumpy dirt driveway. The wind picked up and Reesa tilted her face up towards the sunshine and closed her eyes as she listened to the leaves and pine needles of the trees shift and blow. Creaks of limbs and rustles of squirrels in the undergrowth calmed the last remaining bit of her frazzled nerves. "Yes," she said aloud. "Yes, this is home." She patted the wooden banister of the porch on her way up the steps, and when she opened the creaky door to the cabin, comfort and peace enveloped her like a warm embrace.

~

Theo pulled up outside of Reesa's cabin and stumbled upon an entire flock of hysterical females as they all laughed, tears pouring out of their eyes as Jamie tried to finish whatever story she'd been telling. His grandmother, Reesa, Clare, and Jamie sat along the front porch, each holding a cold beverage of some sort, which he thought he'd take a peek at here soon to see what had them in such a fit. It innocently looked like tea, but he wasn't certain with the way they laughed even harder when they saw his reaction to their behavior.

"Ol' fuddy duddy is here now," Jamie guffawed. "Hey, T.J."

"Dare I even come up there?" he asked.

"Yes, yes, yes." Reesa waved him forward and hopped to her feet from one of the wooden rocking chairs. "I'll get you a glass of tea. And perfect timing." She darted inside and came out a few minutes later with a glass for him. "Billy Lou hired a man to help me build the deck. I was going to try myself, but she found someone who is willing to teach me and help me."

Theo's eyes narrowed on his grandmother. "And who is that?"

Billy Lou sipped her tea, avoiding his gaze.

"Jason Wright." Theo knew immediately, and he didn't like it. His jaw clenched as he held back his argument against his grandmother's idea.

"Can't complain about Mr. Wright," Jamie sassed, fanning her face from a pretend blush. "That gorgeous specimen is coming over tomorrow morning, bright and early, to help Reesa get started. I'm going to bring them coffee." She grinned.

"Jason Wright," Theo stated again in confirmation.

Billy Lou waved her hand. "He's a sweet boy, Theo. Don't give me that look."

"Boy? He's a grown man, Grandma, and he's been divorced twice."

"Oh, those girls weren't right for him, and you know it. Besides, I'm hiring him to help Reesa, not marry her."
"Right..." Theo trailed off.

"*Mr.* Wright," Jamie corrected with a wicked gleam in her eye. Theo huffed his disapproval and sat on the steps next to Clare.

"You don't like him?" Clare asked.

"He's fine," Theo replied. "We just have history."

"History, meaning being the two biggest heartthrobs in Piney!" Jamie giggled. "Only, Jason took full advantage of all the female attention. Ol' T.J. over here played hard to get."

"I didn't *play* anything. I had other things on my mind besides girls."

"Oh, come on now, that is not true. Sophomore year I caught you and Sarah Schaffer kissing under the bleachers," Jamie challenged, pointing her finger at him.

His face turned crimson as the other women laughed, Clare giving him a playful shove in the shoulder that had him laughing and slowly relaxing. "That was one time. A lapse in judgment."

"Sarah walked out with stars in her eyes." Jamie blinked heavenward in dramatic fashion.

"And then wouldn't leave me alone for the next six weeks," Theo reminded her.
"That was so funny too," Jamie chuckled.

His eyes danced with humor as he studied his old friend before looking at Reesa. Her face was lit with glee at listening to their banter and when she caught him staring at her, she wriggled her eyebrows in jest. "Avoid under the bleachers on game nights," he told Clare. "Otherwise, twenty years from now you'll be teased."

"I don't think I have to worry about that." Clare laughed. "Especially after today."

"Why? What happened today?" Reesa asked.

"Oh, Teddy mentioned he's not able to give me a ride to school anymore, at least for a little while."

"What? Why?" Reesa asked. "And how am I just now hearing about this?"

"It's no big deal, Mom." Clare shrugged her shoulders, though all of them could see her feelings were slightly hurt. "He's got a girlfriend now, and she doesn't really like me riding with him every day. I get it."

"Seriously? A girlfriend whined about you?" Reesa asked, her defenses rising. "Who is this girl?"

"Mom, chill." Clare held up her hand and laughed. "It's okay. Teddy may be experiencing one of those lapses in judgments Theo was talking about, but he's a smart guy. I don't think it will last long. In the meantime, I'm going to be cool about it, because he's my friend and I don't want to cause any unnecessary drama for him." She took a sip of her drink. "Oh, and I'll need you to take me to school in the morning." She flashed a chummy smile at her mother.

"I guess I will," Reesa sighed. "Totally ruins my luxurious lifestyle of sleeping in until ten, but I'll sacrifice my ways for you, dear daughter."

"You've never slept in a day in your life," Clare countered.

Reesa winked at her daughter as a car drove up the driveway, the local pizza shop's logo resting on top of a beat-up car. Theo turned to his grandmother in surprise. "What? Can't a woman take a night off every once in a while? Reesa and I thought it best since we had a long day." Billy Lou nodded for Theo to stand and take care of paying for the pizza, which he didn't mind doing, so that none of the women had to get up from where they were sitting. A young man emerged with glasses and a red baseball cap slung over his head, his face showing full-on anxiety when Theo walked towards him. His eyes flashed to behind Theo and landed on Clare. "Hey, Clare."

"Hey, Charlie." She waved, stood, and walked over towards him and Theo. "I didn't know you worked for Jerry's Pizza."

"Yeah, just a couple nights a week. The rest of the time, I'm at the sub sandwich place."

"Two jobs? That's a lot," Clare acknowledged.

The boy shrugged as he handed Theo the pizza and accepted the cash. He began fishing around in a black folder for change.

"Keep the rest as the tip," Theo stated, seeing the surprise cross the boy's face at receiving a twenty-dollar tip from him.

"Thank you, Mr. Whitley. I appreciate that." The nervous boy stashed the cash back into the folder.

"I hope you guys enjoy." His nervous gaze flashed towards Clare again.

She smiled in a friendly manner and waved. "See you tomorrow at school."

"See ya." The boy hurried back to his car and drove away.

"He was cute," Reesa called to her daughter. "Who is he?"

"Just a boy, Mom."

"I believe he thinks she's cute," Jamie chimed in. "Did you see the way he kicked the dirt with his shoe when Clare talked to him? He was shy."

"Okay, let's not make it weird," Clare warned, and Theo turned to her in amusement.

"Do you even realize who you just said that too?" Theo asked, sitting beside her on the steps.

Reesa nudged his back with her shoe as she sat behind him in the rocking chair. "Hey now, Whitley. A little weird is a good thing."

"A lot of weird is not, Mom." Clare pointed to the pizza box. "We opening that or what?"

Theo handed her a box as Reesa walked inside the house to grab paper plates and napkins for everyone and handed them out, grabbing the box from Clare and walking to each person so they could help themselves to the pizza inside.

"Honey, you keep your eyes open. Even a shy, sweet boy like Charlie has potential. He works hard, bless his heart, but I hear he is one of the smartest kids at that school."

"That is definitely true," Clare reported. "He's in my chemistry class and everyone wants to be his partner in lab. We were partners the other day; that's how I've gotten to know him. He's nice, but of course high school diplomacy dictates that you can only talk to him under such circumstances, or you will be labeled and branded as a nerd too."

"Good thing you hate labels, right?" Reesa asked.

"Ugh, they're so stupid," Clare agreed. "The great thing about being the new kid is that I can pretty much talk to anyone, and no one really says anything because they give you that 'she needs to find her clique' time. Now, once I actually choose my friends, I'm sure I will be labeled, but I'm hoping I can keep people guessing and just have friends from all the cliques. Everyone knows I'm friends with Teddy, but I don't think they've really figured me out yet." Clare pointed at her mom,

"But I have yet to win the favor of the cheerleaders. Sorry, Mom."

"You were a cheerleader?" Jamie asked in surprise as Reesa rolled her eyes.

"Only for a couple of years."

"Yeah, until she got pregnant with me," Clare clarified. "I threw off her cute little cheer body."

Reesa laughed. "Hey, I still looked cute, just in a different way."

Theo liked that Clare and Reesa could openly talk about Reesa's youth and pregnancy days without Clare feeling as if her mother regretted the situation. There was equal respect between the two as they bantered back and forth.

"Did you fall for the star football player?" Jamie asked.

Reesa shook her head. "Absolutely not. I have my pride." She laughed as she nodded towards the empty driveway. "It was the local boy who worked multiple jobs. The smart boy who would go on to become a pediatrician of all things."

"My dad's a doctor?" Clare asked, the news hitting her with surprise.

"Last I heard," Reesa explained.

"Very cool."

"Do you want to be a doctor one day, Clare?" Jamie asked.

"Absolutely not." Clare shook her head. "I just like the idea that I might have good science genes in here." She tapped her brain. "Because chemistry is hard, but maybe I'll be great at Biology or Anatomy next year."

Reesa smiled as Clare draped her arm around Theo's shoulders, surprising him as she gave him a squeeze. "So, big guy, what do you say about being my ride tomorrow morning?"

"Clare!" Reesa's lyrical laugh made him smirk. "I said I would take you."

"Yeah, but you're working on uploading your newest pattern, and you have the hot carpenter coming over, *and* it's sort of on Theo's way to work in the morning..." Clare waited for his response and Theo nodded.

"I guess I can do that."

"Great." Clare went back to her pizza. "At least with you I won't be late." Reesa tossed her last piece of crust at her daughter, pelting her in the back as Billy Lou and Jamie laughed.

"Watch it, teenager." Reesa tapped her toe against Theo's back until he turned to face her. "Thank you, though. I do have to upload that pattern in the morning before the deck guy—"

"Mr. Wright!" Jamie interrupted.

"Jason Wright," Reesa added for her friend's amusement. "Gets here."

"It's not a problem," Theo assured her. "I can bring her home too, if she doesn't mind hanging out at the garage for an hour or so." He looked at Clare and she shrugged.

"I can do my homework there," she told her mom, and Reesa nodded that she was fine with that.

"If you're okay with that, I'm okay with it." Reesa looked to Theo again.

"It's fine," Theo assured her. "She's not as annoying as some people."

"I'll pretend not to be offended." Reesa's lips tilted upward as she handed him the sketch book of Billy Lou's deck design. "Here's our project."

"Our?" he asked.

Reesa motioned a thumb between herself and Billy Lou. "I did not realize how talented this lovely lady is."

Billy Lou waved away the compliment with a slight blush. "I just adore design in all aspects of life. Clothes, crafts, lawns, gardens..."

"This looks like a bit more than just a deck." Theo looked up at his grandmother. "A pergola too?"

"Well, yes. You know as well as I do that in the summer that sun just beats down back there. This way, Reesa and Clare can have a nice place to sit outside even when it's hot. And they'll have the partial shade needed to grow some pretty flowers. Otherwise, not one pot will bloom on that porch back there."

He grunted that he understood as he flipped the page to look at the drafted construction plans his grandmother had put together as well. It'd been years since she'd gotten to draw up a building project, the last being the outdoor entertainment area at her own house. She and his grandfather had just completed the project when he passed, and the space had only been used once since then. "Looks good."

"I'm going to learn how to build a deck," Reesa reminded everyone. "I can't wait. I've built furniture before." Clare snorted and Reesa feigned offense. "Hey now, it was good."

"Not the first piece. She made me a bed frame when I was like eight. The first night, my mattress fell through the frame onto the floor."

"I didn't quite have my measurements right," Reesa admitted. "But I learned my lesson."

"You did get better," Clare encouraged. "The bottom drawer on my dresser is only *slightly* crooked."

Reesa motioned as if that was proof enough that she'd improved.

"Well, now you will learn from Jason." Billy Lou patted Reesa's knee. "He's a nice man and should be rather patient with you. He knows I've hired him to help you learn as well as help get the structure up. But his first priority is to teach you. He seemed open to the idea."

"I bet he did," Theo mumbled, Jamie giving a quiet snicker in agreement.

"Theodore James, now stop that now," Billy Lou warned. "I'm not playing matchmaker for Reesa. I hired the man to do a job." Theo opened his mouth to speak but his grandmother cut him off. "And I would have asked you to do it, but you're too busy at the garage to have this project on your plate too."

"And you're carting my daughter to school," Reesa pointed out. "I think you're helping enough already."

"I'm not *that* difficult," Clare teased. "Or am I?" She raised a mischievous eyebrow at him and grinned.

"Now that is *Inconceivable*!" Theo's voice hitched into a different tone as he tugged on Clare's ponytail before he stood, smiling down at their baffled faces.

"He did it!" Clare hollered on a laugh. "He actually did it!"

Theo shook his head. "I don't know what you're talking about," he said, pretending nonchalance. "I'll swing by in the morning to pick you up for school."

"Don't you even think about it." Clare motioned towards her mother. "You just—"

Reesa stood and walked down the front steps with him, linking her arm through his. He didn't tug away, he didn't flinch, he didn't even turn at the sound of Clare blubbering in stunned surprise at him actually quoting a movie in conversation. "I'm impressed, Theo." Reesa lightly leaned her temple against his arm as they walked. "You've completely shocked my teenager. I wasn't sure anyone could do that other than myself."

"I'm just full of surprises." Theo's sarcasm had her laughing as they reached his truck and she relinquished her hold on his arm and instead slid her arm around his waist for a light squeeze, tucking herself against him.

"Thank you."

"You're welcome." He looked down at her, her face upturned to his, the witching hour settling upon her creamy skin and highlighting her dark hair with a golden sheen. He hesitated a moment, liking the way she fit against him and how easy it seemed to have her there. "Have fun with your new project tomorrow."

"I will." Her eyes searched his and she lifted onto her tiptoes and grazed a light kiss on his jawline beneath his cheek. His grip around her body tightened a moment as he debated whether or not to dive headfirst into testing the waters. But then he remembered the audience on the porch, and he reminded himself he barely knew her, and he thought about how he'd sworn he didn't want any sort of romantic relationship at the moment. But all of those thoughts seemed to fall flat when staring down at her. "See you tomorrow morning."

"But for now, rest well and dream of large women." Reesa patted a hand against his chest as she stepped away. His shock at her statement made her laugh. "Look, Theo, if you're going to quote The Princess Bride, you better know it all." She winked at him as he slid behind the wheel of his truck. "See ya tomorrow." Tapping his window seal, she backed away from his truck as he shifted toward home.

CHAPTER TEN

Okay, so Jamie wasn't lying when she said Jason Wright was a handsome guy. He was. He was tall, lean, and chiseled. He made Captain America look like second place in a national pageant. However, Reesa also found he had an easygoing, fun personality which made him seem like even a better catch. She wasn't sure what his story was or why he'd had bad luck with his relationships, but Jamie had already texted her that she would be arriving to provide coffee and an early lunch for the two of them so as to "sneak a peek of him in a tool belt." Reesa had yet to feel a thrill or rush of attraction towards the man, but she enjoyed his company, and he was patient in his teaching. Her cell phone rang and curious as to why Theo would be calling her mid-morning, she held up a finger for Jason to pause in his explanation over framing. "Good morning, Theo, to what do I owe this pleasure?"

"Hey." Theo's voice sent a small buzz of warmth through her, but she tamped it down so as not to give herself away to Jason. And because she was still trying to convince herself that she was crazy for even thinking Theo could be more than a friend. "How's it going?"

"Good." Reesa leaned back in the deck chair and waited for him to give her the real reason why he called.

"I forgot what time Clare gets out of school."

"Ah." Reesa babbled off the release time, but she didn't think that was the real reason for his call. He was quiet. Too quiet. And he went to the same high school. Surely the release schedule hadn't changed that much over the years. He would at least have some idea of the time. "Is that all you needed?" Again, silence lingered on the phone before an annoyed sigh filtered through.

"I was just checking on you," Theo admitted, and she could tell he hated doing it, which made her smile.

"I see. Well, Jason is just teaching me all I need to know to build a magnificent structure. I'm learning that without lateral bracing, my pergola can just sway in the wind and blow away if too big a storm blows through… which he informs me, happens often. And that if we attach sections of rail in between pergola posts that will strengthen the pergola. Installing 45-degree bracing in between the post and header beam also will increase stability. And we will be using 6x6s for support posts which will further strengthen it. This sucker isn't going anywhere. Though now, instead of a pergola, I kind of want it to be a covered deck and porch, so he's helping me draft that idea as well." She paused a minute. "How'd you like that? I sound like I know what I'm talking about, don't I?"

She could hear the light hint of a smile in his voice. "Yeah, you do. Sounds like it is going well, then."

"It is. Billy Lou is going to swing by in a bit and see what new ideas we have drafted up and then we will go from there. Really right now we are just measuring out the space."

"Well, I'll let you get back to it, then."

"Thanks for checking up on me." Reesa muttered her goodbyes and hung up, setting her phone aside. "Sorry about that. Neighborhood watch making sure all is okay."

Jason smirked. "T.J. knows I'm helping you?"

She nodded. "Why?"

"I'm just surprised he doesn't seem to mind."

"Why do you say that?"

"He and I go way back," Jason said. "We tended to have the same taste in girls." He smirked.

"Well, we aren't dating, so I don't see why he would care who I'm working with."

"You're not dating?" Jason asked, nodding towards her phone. "But he was calling to check on you?"

"He's sort of one of three people I actually know here, and he's been sweet to help my daughter and me get situated."

Jason's dimples flashed a minute as he chuckled. "Right. Well, let's get the tape measure and some string, and we'll rope off our area. Sound good?"

"Yes. Let's get to it. I want to have it up before Billy Lou arrives so she can envision the space and make the call on what we do moving forward." Reesa walked with him over to the back porch.

"Are you going to paint it or stain it?"

"Probably stain it. I mean, we would want it to blend with the cabin I would think."

He studied the old house and grimaced. "Yeah, that cabin needs a new coat of protectant on it. Otherwise, you'll just be trying to match the color of rot."

"Is that something you do?"

"No, but I have a guy."

"Good. I love this little place. I want to make sure we take care of it."

"I'll mention it to Mrs. Whitley and see if she wants me to line that up. It'd be good to do that all at once when the deck is finished. Because you may have to replace some boards on the house, sand some down, and then re-stain the whole place. Then everything could match."

"I don't want it to look too new, though." Reesa leaned her weight on her right leg as she crossed her arms over her chest and stared at the quaint cabin. "I like that it looks old."

"It can still look that way, just have some repairs done. Otherwise in a year or two, you're going to have a bigger mess on your hands."

"Alright..." Reesa turned a sly smile on him, and his left brow rose in response.

"What?"

"How are you at building porch swings?"

He laughed. "Not my wheelhouse. I can do it, I just don't. I mostly focus on framing houses, barns, and decks. But—"

"Let me guess, you know a guy?" Reesa grinned as he laughed.

"As a matter of fact, I do." Jason leaned towards her, his eyes dancing in flirtation as Jamie rounded the side of the house with her hands full carrying a cardboard cup holder with four cups of coffee and a box of some culinary creations she'd picked up as well. She paused when she spotted them, and a knowing smile spread across her face as to what she'd just interrupted.

"Hey guys! Jason, it's so good to see you!" She handed him a cup of coffee and he took it with a friendly toast towards her as he walked away from the two of them to fish around in his toolbox for his tape measure. Jamie gave a little shimmy with her shoulders as she waltzed her way towards Reesa. "Girl," she whispered. "He is looking *good*."

"Shhh," Reesa warned. "You don't want him to hear you."

"And what was that?" Jamie bounced her fingers between Reesa and Jason. "Did I interrupt a little flirtatious tryst happening?"

Reesa rolled her eyes. "Don't be ridiculous. We were just talking about the deck."

"Mmhmm." Jamie set the box of pastries on a wooden stump by the current porch railing and watched the man walk towards them. "He moves like a sexy lion on the prowl. Oh my."

"*Jamie,*" Reesa hissed, staring at her friend in shock. A nervous, bubbly laugh escaped her lips as he approached and as if he knew what they were discussing, flashed a killer smile.

"Ready?" He held up his tape measure.

"Yep." Reesa motioned for Jamie to have a seat and get comfortable, her friend not hesitating a moment.

Between the first and second round of measurements, Billy Lou arrived and joined Jamie on the back porch, the two women watching Reesa's interactions with Jason closely. Reesa began tying off the last of the surveying string, Jason walking up to help. His fingers brushed over hers as he took over the task and she quickly moved out of the way to let him finish. She saw Jamie's amused smirk at her actions and felt a blush stain her cheeks.

"I'm going to pretend you didn't hire Jason to nudge Theo into asking her out, but are you sure it was a good idea?" Jamie whispered to Billy Lou.

"Now, Jamie, why on Earth would I do such a thing like that?" Billy Lou asked, her eyes wide. Her feigned innocence was fleeting, though, and Jamie giggled.

"You are bad, Billy Lou. Just straight up bad."

"I can't help it. You've seen the two of them together. Theodore cannot let Reesa slip through his fingers. She is precious and just in the short time she's been here, I have seen that boy relax, smile, laugh, and serve in ways I haven't seen in years. It's like she's awakened him from some sort of stagnant and lonely slumber and is slowly bringing him out of his shell. He needs this." Billy Lou motioned towards Reesa as she and Jason discussed numbers and joists.

"I don't disagree," Jamie agreed. "But I don't know if Reesa is even looking for a relationship. She doesn't seem too focused on herself. Everything is about Clare."

"I can't fault her there," Billy Lou admitted. "But I've also seen a change in her as well. She's come to depend on Theodore in ways that flirt with the line between friendship and relationship. The two of them will have to own up to it here soon and figure it out. It's not fair to either of them to live in limbo like that. So, if a handsome, available bachelor needs to be thrown in as a plot twist to get the ball moving, then I'll pencil him in."

"You think T.J. will come home early from work?"
"Oh, honey, I'm betting on it."

Jamie hooted as Billy Lou lightly fluffed her hair and smiled. "He won't be able to stand it."

~

Clare glanced up from her Chemistry textbook as Theo entered his office and slid into his desk chair. He tapped on the keyboard of his computer, hit print, and an older gentleman walked inside. Theo handed him the invoice and the man grunted his approval. He then handed Theo his credit card, Theo quickly and efficiently taking payment and sending the man on his way. No words were exchanged, just a quick and clean transaction for his hard work. The older man tapped the edge of his cap towards Clare on his way out and she offered a friendly smile. When the door closed, Theo penciled something on his desk calendar. "So... is that your typical customer experience?" Clare asked.

Theo glanced up. "Pretty much. Why?"

"You didn't even tell him thank you."

"He knows."

"Does he?" Clare asked, doubtful.

"He's been coming here for years, so I'd say he's pretty familiar with how things go."
"You grunt. He grunts. Grunt, grunt, grunt, and then he leaves. It's like caveman customer service."

Theo sighed and leaned back in his chair. Clare held up her hands to ward off a potential bad mood. "Just an observation. That's all."

"And how would you have handled it?" Theo asked.

"Well," She closed her Chemistry book and set it aside. "I would have said, "Alright, Mr. Grunt, we did a carburetor swap and an oil change for you today. That comes to such and such amount." Clare pretended to accept a credit card with a smile and air swiped it. "Just sign here. Let me print your invoice for you right quick. We appreciate you trusting us with your vehicle. You let us know if there's anything else you need. Okay? Have a great day." She lifted a sheet of paper and handed it to Theo with a sweet smile. "And end scene."

Theo sat, amused at how similar Clare was to Reesa. He crossed his arms and leaned back in his chair. "You're hired. When can you start?"

Clare laughed and then realized he was serious and her face sobered. "Wait, what?"

"Want a job? You could work after school and on Saturdays if you want."

"Seriously?"

"Do I look like I'm kidding?" Theo asked.

"I don't know. You look like you always do, which makes it hard to tell. You don't exactly have a wide range of emotional expression, you know."

"I'm serious," he confirmed for her. "You can think about it and let me know." He clicked off the computer and motioned for her to follow him to his truck.

She gathered up her textbook and backpack, slipping it inside. As they walked to his truck, she asked, "So what's the pay?"

He hadn't thought that far ahead, but he considered it a moment. "Eleven an hour."

"Wow," he heard her whisper, and he bit back a grin as they climbed into his truck.

"Okay, I'm in." Clare held out her hand. "But with a few conditions."

"Shoot," he offered with a wave of his hand for her to lay them out.

"I don't work on Fridays. That way, if there's some sort of teenage festivity, like a ball game or dance, I can go."

"Okay."

"And what if I want a Saturday off to do something with Mom, how do I request that?"

"You just tell me." Theo shrugged as if the answer was simple.

"But what if I end up taking a lot of Saturdays off? Would that be annoying?"

"No."

"You sure?"

"Clare, I don't have anyone working the desk. You'd be a bonus. But if you aren't there, I can handle it myself. It's not going to bother me. What will bother me is if you completely neglect the job when you're actually at the job."

"I think that's fair." She beamed at him. "Mom's going to be excited. I mean, I help her with her business stuff occasionally, but I get room and board for that help."

"Seems fair," Theo pointed out.

Laughing, Clare agreed. "Thanks, Theo. I'm looking forward to helping you out."

"I do have one question for you," Theo mentioned.

"What's that?"

"When you acted out your scene, did you know a carburetor swap was actually a real thing?"

Clare's eyes widened. "No way?!"

He chuckled at her shock.

"I was just trying to use car jargon. Man, I'm good. See? I'm already learning the lingo. I'll watch all the fifty-five Fast and Furious movies and then I'll be a walking encyclopedia of car knowledge."

"Right... because that is definitely the kind of person someone wants to be working on their car."

"I won't be working on the cars," Clare pointed out. "Just chatting about them."

"Please don't."

She flashed a wide smile and he winked at her as they turned into the driveway to the cabin. "Guess Jason's gone for the day."

"Much to your relief," Clare muttered.

"I have no problem with Jason."

"But you would have a problem with him if he hit on my mom." He sat quietly a minute before starting to respond, but she held up her hand to stop him from speaking. "Don't worry, your secret is safe with me."

"I don't have secrets. And no, I wouldn't have a problem with him hitting on your mom. I would have a problem with him hitting on any woman. He's not a standup guy, no matter what people think."

"Well, Jamie seemed to like him."

"She likes the look of him, as do most women. But looks and personality can be drastically different."

"Is this you subtly warning me so that I will warn my mom against him."

"No. I don't play those games. This is me stating the facts. You and your mom can do what you want with them."

"And if she decided to ignore those facts?" Clare asked curiously.

"Then that's her choice."

"And you'd be okay with it?" she prodded.

"Wouldn't I have to be?"

Clare fell quiet as he parked under the shade of the woods. "No," she finally answered. "Because my mom is worth fighting over. I can tell you like her. I'm not blind. And you can deny it all you want," Her voice hardened at the thought of him disliking Reesa in any way. "But if you like her and she started dating someone else and you just passively let it happen because you just didn't want to interfere or whatever, then you don't deserve her. She's worth putting yourself out there. She's worth waiting for. She's worth every second you can give her, because she's amazing. And when she decides to befriend, like, or love someone, she goes all in. It doesn't matter what past you have or anything. She takes people as they are and who they want to be. She's worth every ounce of grit you have if you want to be with her."

"You're forgetting part of the equation, Clare."

"Me?" she asked.

"No, me. I may have contemplated pursuing your mom, but if the feelings aren't reciprocated, I don't waste my time. I'm her friend, yes, and that's what it is right now. I'm not going to push for more if there's nothing on the other side."

"Can I ask you something... even if it makes you mad?" He inhaled a deep breath and she grimaced. "Which I can tell I'm already flirting the line of making you upset, but one more question?"

"One more. That's it," Theo agreed, uncomfortable with their conversation.

"If I weren't in the picture, would you have already asked her out?"

His eyes widened in surprise at her question. "No, hy would you think that?" His voice rose and a relieved smile washed over her face.

"Just checking. I didn't think that was the case, but it has been in the past with other men. I don't like the idea of my mom not having a chance with someone she cares about because of me."

"I haven't known your mom long enough yet to know if I want to ask her out. I don't date much." He flushed at admitting that to a teenager. "But when I do, it's usually with someone I've known longer than a couple weeks."

"Why?"

He narrowed his eyes at her.

"Ah…" She looked out the windshield. "I've hit my quota of questions, right? Sorry. I don't always know when to turn them off."

"I don't like messing up," Theo admitted. "And let's just say I play along with your idea that I like your mom—"

"Idea?" Clare rolled her eyes in the stereotypical teenager method but waved for him to continue.

"If I asked her out, she said yes, we dated, and then something went wrong, what then? We're neighbors. My grandmother is your landlord. That would make things uncomfortable for everyone. And I don't want to do that to you and your mom. I also do not want to make things harder for my grandmother. She likes the two of you and loves having you in the cabin. I don't want to jeopardize that for her, so there's that to consider."

"I get it." Clare rubbed her chin in thought and then looked at him again. "But I think you're totally missing out on the possibility of something great. Who cares how long you've known us? And if things go south, then you act like grownups and just deal with it. My mom's first instinct will be to leave and move somewhere else. That's just how she's lived her life. We've moved all over the place for fun and for necessity, depending on the situation. But we have never made such deep connections with people as quickly as we have here. You, Billy Lou, Jamie, Teddy. We don't want to leave. So, if it doesn't work out, you can both suck it up so we can stay. I'll even play the 'me' card. For Clare's sake, it will work out no matter what. If you date or if you don't, for Clare's sake, life in Piney will be good and permanent."

Theo extended his hand towards her, and she surveyed the gesture a moment before placing hers in his and shaking hands. A small smile tilted the corner of her lips. "Let's go see how much damage Dreamy McCarpenter has done to your chances, shall we?"

Exasperated, Theo released her hand and climbed out of his truck to the sound of Clare's amused giggle.

CHAPTER ELEVEN

Clare led the way around the house following the sounds of female laughter, and Theo followed suit. "What? No deck?" Clare asked, stepping up onto the small back porch and finding a seat on the steps.

"A work in progress." Reesa handed her daughter a graphed notebook that contained sketches and measurements. "It's been a busy day."

Billy Lou looked up at Theo, shading her eyes to see him. "And how was your day, honey?"

Clare hopped to her feet, draped an elbow on his shoulder and beamed. "His day was fantastic, because he has a new employee."

Reesa's smile faltered at her daughter's news, and she looked at Theo's somewhat entertained expression as her daughter chummily elbowed his side. "Theo offered me a job at his shop to run the office desk."

"Oh." Reesa's lack of enthusiasm caused Clare's face to fall.

"What? You don't want me to?" she asked, curious as to why her mom would not be just as excited for her.

"It's just... it's not exactly the kind of place I'd like for you to work."

Theo's shoulders straightened. "Kind of place?" His tone fell flat and hard and Reesa sighed.

"Not that it's bad, Theo. It's just... working with a bunch of grown men? It doesn't scream safe to me."

"Ah." Theo considered it a moment. "Well, I'm always there. I'd keep an eye out for her. And the other men are fine. I know you don't care for Mike, but he's not a bad guy. Plus, I have cameras around the place and in the office."

"Come on, Mom," Clare begged. "At least let me try it. If I get the weirdo vibes from anyone, I'll tell Theo and you and that can be that. But at least let me give it a go. It'd just be after school and *some* Saturdays." She eyed Theo on her last remark, and he nodded, bringing the smile back to her face. "We've been negotiating."

Billy Lou looked pleased, and Reesa turned to her. "You think it would be safe for her there?"

"Absolutely," Billy Lou agreed. "Theodore runs a tight ship."

Giving in, Reesa nodded. "Fine. You can try it."

"Woohoo!" Clare danced and raised a hand for Theo to high five and he did so reluctantly. She elbowed him again. "Come on, act like you're excited. It was your idea in the first place!"

Reesa's brows lifted and surprise lit her eyes. "Really?"

Theo nudged Clare away from him as he walked towards a free chair and sat. "She has a knack for customer service, and apparently finds mine lacking."

Reesa bit her lip at his obvious confusion over how someone could think him not capable of friendly customer service, but she only nodded. "That she does. Thanks for giving her an opportunity. I hope she realizes how special it is."

Reesa eyed her daughter and Clare nodded that she did.

"The first thing I'm going to do is clean that place. Everything is covered in grease." Clare pulled a twisted face.

Chuckling, Billy Lou patted Theo's arm. "Sounds like she will be a much-needed force at the garage."

"Perhaps so. We will see."

"He's thrilled by the idea; he's just playing it cool." Clare looked at Reesa and her mom nodded towards the house.

"Why don't you go put your backpack away?"

"On it." Clare happily drummed her hands on Theo's shoulder as she passed by him, and the older two women grinned at her enthusiasm.

When the cabin door closed, Reesa cornered Theo. "Are you sure about this?"

"Yes."

"And you're sure there will be no trouble with the other men there?"

"I'm sure. And it's as flexible as you need it to be."

"Thanks."

"So, what did you get accomplished today with the amazing Jason?" His sarcastic tone had Billy Lou swatting his knee.

"He's a good teacher." Reesa pointed towards their flags and survey string. "We mapped out the area. We decided to go with flush beam since we plan to add the pergola. I learned about drip caps, deck ledgers, and the difference between drop beam and flush. So yeah, pretty soon I'll be a master apprentice. *And* much to Jamie's disappointment, I made it through the entire day without falling in love with Mr. Wright or being asked out, so I would say it was a win."

Billy Lou smiled at the serious expression on her grandson's face as he listened. At Reesa's last remark, he nodded his approval. "Good. And were you here all day?" he asked Billy Lou.

"She and Jamie supervised." Reesa used her fingers to add air-quotes around the last word and Billy Lou fluffed a hand to her hair.

"Well, someone has to make sure everything runs smoothly."

"And to drool," Reesa pointed out.

Guffawing, Billy Lou didn't even blush. "Honey, I just left that up to Jamie."

"True. She had that covered." Reesa smiled. "Jamie's coming back for supper. Want to join us?" she looked to Theo, and he shook his head.

"No, thanks. I'm pretty beat today." He stood to leave. "I'm a bit talked out."

"Clare chat your ear off?" Reesa stood to follow him. "I'll be right back, Billy Lou."

"Take your time, honey. I'm going to get me a refill of tea." She walked her way through the back door and into the cabin, completely at ease, and Reesa smiled at her back. When she turned back to Theo, he stood studying her, his brow furrowed, and a scowl on his face. "Is something wrong?"

He shook his head. "No."

"Are you sure? Because you're standing there like you either want to yell at me or pummel me."

"I don't want to do either of those things," he assured her. "I'm just reading you."

"Reading me?" Reesa, intrigued, crossed her arms over her chest and tilted her head. "And what, pray tell, are you reading?" She took a step towards him. "Gauging whether or not I fell for Mr. Wright's charms?"

"No."

She tapped her chin. "Hmm... whether or not I'm offended you won't stay for supper?"

"No." Theo's hands rested in his pockets as he turned to go.

She followed after him and grinned at the long-suffering sigh she heard escape his lips at her pestering him. "Whether or not I'm okay with Clare working for you?"

"No." He glanced over his shoulder briefly as he continued towards his truck. "Now stop. I'm leaving." He opened his truck door and Reesa slid between him and his seat so he could not escape. "Reesa, I really am tired today."

"I can see that, but you can't tell a girl that you're reading her and then not tell her why or how or what you're reading about her. That's not very fair. And now I'm inwardly freaking out that you're upset with me in some way."

"Why would I be upset with you?" he asked.

"I don't know, you tell me." Reesa motioned for him to continue. "That's just where my mind goes when someone seems disappointed in me."

"Who said I was disappointed?"

"Well, you didn't say it." Reesa pointed out. "But you said you were reading me and then you looked annoyed and then you walked away, so I'm assuming you are disappointed or aggravated."

"I'm not either of those things. I was just trying to gauge how you were doing."

"Why?"

"Because it was a long day for you to be forced into a matchmaking scenario. It was a wellness check, that's all."

Her eyes widened. "Matchmaking? You mean Billy Lou intended for Jason and I to hit it off?"

"Probably," Theo admitted.

"Hm, that explains some things." Reesa looked up at him. "I assure you I did not fall victim to the dreamy carpenter's ways. He is nice, though, and should deserve some credit for that."

"Duly noted." Theo gently grabbed her elbow and moved her out of his way so he could climb into his truck. "I'm sad you won't stay for supper. Clare will be bummed too. But I get it. Guess I've just gotten used to having you around." She shrugged and hated to admit that she also liked having him around. She'd keep that to herself for now.

"You'll see me tomorrow."

"I will?"
"I'm taking Clare to school, right?"

"Oh." Reesa considered his offer. "I didn't think about it for tomorrow."

"I don't mind."

"No, I'll take her. Then I can grab coffee on the way back here to work with Jason. Besides, you'll be bringing her home, right? After you close up the garage?"

"I would assume so, unless you wanted to pick her up for some reason."

"No, that works out well. I just don't want to take advantage of your willingness to cart her around."

"You aren't. I'm offering."

"Still..." Reesa nibbled her bottom lip. "Theo?" He unbuckled his seat belt, stepped back out of his truck, and closed the door. He motioned for her to walk back towards the house. "Oh, are you staying now?" Reesa couldn't help the smile that lit her face.

"It would seem I don't have a choice."

"Okay, yay!" Reesa linked her arm in his and briefly rested her head against his bicep. A loud cracking sound boomed through the trees and they both stopped in their tracks. "What was that?" Reesa asked, slipping behind Theo as if a bear might jump out of the woods.

Theo peered through the tree line as they heard a thud and a rustle of leaves. "A tree limb snapped."

"That sounded like a gun shot. Wow." Reesa placed a hand on her heart. "Are you sure?" She peeked around him, and he looked down at her in amusement.

"You okay back there, scaredy cat?"

Straightening, she ran her hands through her hair and tugged the hemline of her shirt to pull herself together. "I'm fine. That was just... new. That's all."

"You were scared."

"I was not."

"You were," he challenged.

"Maybe a little. But I don't have my mace on me. I feel invincible with that stuff. As you well know." She waved towards his face, and she smiled, briefly brushing her fingers over his stubbled cheek. "I see you're growing back the beard."

"Not sure yet." Theo walked to the front door and opened it to Clare and Billy Lou playing a hand of cards.

"I thought you were leaving?" Billy Lou asked.

"I was."

"But he decided to stay because he missed me," Reesa exaggerated. She leaned up on her tiptoes and kissed his cheek. "Isn't that right, Theo?"

He looked heavenward as Billy Lou and Clare shared hopeful glances.

"Okay," Reesa clapped her hands. "I'm going to get started on supper. You're staying too, right, Billy Lou?"

"Oh, I'd love to, honey, but I've got Bridge tonight. You three have fun." She stood, folding her hand of cards on the table. She kissed Theo's other cheek and gave him a quick wink before walking herself out.

"Well, that was a quick exit." Reesa shrugged. "I was thinking of making some fried pork chops. Does that sound good?"

Clare lifted Billy Lou's cards and handed them to Theo. He took a seat with a nod. "Sure."

A cell phone ding buzzed through the air, followed by another and another. It didn't stop for a full minute until Reesa hurried over to the counter where she'd plugged her phone in to charge. She looked at the screen. "Clare, hurry, get the laptop. It's live and people are starting to comment!" She jumped up and down in excitement, Theo watching them curiously as Clare bolted from her chair and down the hall, coming back quickly to set up the laptop on the table. She typed in a website, and Reesa's face popped up on the screen, along with crocheted projects and patterns. "Susan Henkel from Massachusetts says she can't wait to start this and will be tonight!" Clare read.

Reesa rushed around the kitchen gathering supplies for supper and opened a small notebook that sat on her counter. She read the ingredients she'd copied from Billy Lou's cookbook and rushed to the pantry as Clare read another review of her newest pattern.

"What is happening right now?" Theo asked, the two girls excited when Reesa's phone continued to ding.

"I'm sorry. I'm vain," Reesa admitted. "On release day, when I release a new pattern, I like to have my phone notify me when someone leaves a review for it, or a comment about it. Makes me feel good that so many people love it." She blushed at admitting she liked the approval of other people, but it was her work she was most excited about. People loved her patterns almost as much as she did, and she'd worked hard on this last one. She looked to Clare.

"Grace Tennison says, 'Another genius pattern by the incredible Reesa!'"

"Oh, yes! Grace commented? Wow!" Reesa did a small jig in the kitchen as Clare scrolled some more on the computer.

Her daughter briefly looked up at Theo. "Grace is a big deal in the crochet world."

Reesa slit open the meat package with shaky hands, her excitement making her giddy and clumsy. She attempted to slow down, but the positive reviews and shared thrill continued to pour in. She'd just scooped some flour into a bowl when Theo walked up beside her and took the cup from her hands. "Go. I'll do this." He tilted his head towards Clare. "Go. Read them all. You two do that. I'll make supper."

"Theo, I—"

"Reesa, it's a good day. A good moment. Enjoy it." He nudged her away from the counter and took over, her eyes misting over at the gesture as she rushed to her daughter's side to read over her shoulder.

She gasped at the glowing response to her pattern and the number of sales that had already come through. Her hopes of buying Clare a car for her sixteenth birthday were slowly coming to fruition. She looked up as Theo washed his hands from battering the chops and she hurried towards him. Grabbing his hand, she tugged him towards the hallway, his reluctant steps fueling her further. "Come on! I'll show you." They entered her bedroom and she walked over to the shelving unit she'd built herself, the uneven shelves perfect for storing some of her former projects. She tugged a chair from her vanity over and stood on top to reach above the highest shelf. Theo walked over, his eyes perusing the bright colors and different patterns and textures that graced the shelves. Reesa tugged and a big, folded mass fell into her arms. She lost her balance on the chair and jumped the remaining distance to the floor before she could fall. Theo caught her elbow before she could stumble onto the floor and the chair toppled over.

"Phew! Good save. This—" She flipped the blanket out in full and let it spread over the floor. "This is the pattern I just released this morning." She stood proudly over it and pointed at different aspects. "It's sort of a mixture of overlay mosaic and granny square techniques. It gives it a vintage feel with unlimited possibilities for pattern users. I went bold with this one because I made it for Clare. She doesn't know that yet, but this is meant for her. All the money from this pattern's sales will go towards buying her a car. I thought it would be a fun surprise. What do you think?" She looked up at Theo and saw the admiration in his eyes.

"Wow. You *made* this?"

"Yep." She beamed, quickly gathering up the corners to fold it back up. "Fresh off the hook." She motioned to a jar holding several crochet hooks nestled amongst the rolls of yarn on the middle shelf. "Blanket patterns are time consuming. I've been working on this one for a while, so my followers have been eager to get their hands on it. I think that will really drive sales." The house phone rang, and Reesa motioned for them to head back to the kitchen. Clare stood by the phone, the receiver to her ear, her face devoid of color. Her eyes, round and nervous, glanced at Reesa. "Mom," She looked at Theo and then back to Reesa. "It's your dad."

Reesa froze, her eyes on Clare as her daughter held out the phone towards her.

"Well?" Theo whispered.

Reesa looked up at him, her emotions evident on her face. He walked over to the phone and took it from Clare's hand, covering the mouthpiece with his palm. "You mailed the letter. They must have gotten it today. Take it as a good sign that he's calling right away." He held it out to her.

Tears flooded her eyes as she took a deep breath and nodded. "Can you take Clare outside?"

Theo motioned for Clare to follow him out the back door and her daughter didn't hesitate to obey. When they were gone, Reesa prayed a silent prayer for strength.

"Hello."

~

"What do you think he's saying to her?" Clare asked as soon as the door closed. "Do you think he's being nice? Yelling at her? Crying?"

"I don't know," Theo admitted, taking the first chair he came across. "We'll find out soon enough."

"Why did they have to call tonight? She was so happy. Her pattern is doing phenomenal. The best she's ever had happen and then this..." She nervously paced the porch. "What if they're mean to her?"

"Clare," Theo waved for her to stop frantically pounding along the porch and to sit by him. "Your mom will be fine no matter how that conversation is going because she has you and me here. If it goes well, we'll celebrate with her. If it goes sour, then we'll be with her. Simple."

Clare lunged at him, wrapping her arms around him and burying her head in his chest as she burst into tears. Surprised, perplexed, and way out of his comfort zone, Theo just stood a moment as the teen relinquished what had to be a lifetime of tears all over the front of his shirt. Gently, he brushed a hand over her ponytail. "Why are you crying? We don't even know how it's going in there yet."

"B-because..." Clare blubbered. "W-w-what if they don't want to s-see h-her?"

Theo wrapped his arms around the girl and tried to soothe her with quiet shushing sounds. "It's going to be alright. Trust me."

"B-but what if th-they don't like me?"

There it was, he thought. The real worry seeping through. His heart ached for Clare. That she carried such a burden or thought made him question whether or not her grandparents even deserved a chance to know her. But it wasn't his parents, and it wasn't his decision. It was Reesa's. All he could do was ensure Clare that, no matter the outcome, she had him. And Billy Lou, of course. "Are you kidding? Who wouldn't like you?"

She sniffled, the sobbing growing quieter as she listened to him. "You're a great kid. You're smart, friendly, and only slightly annoying." He felt her sniff back a laugh. "And you've got an incredible relationship with your mom, who also happens to be a pretty amazing person. If your grandparents don't want to see two people like that, then they're just stupid. And sometimes you just can't help stupid. Besides, their loss is our gain." He patted her back as he spotted movement out of the corner of his eye. He turned his head to see Reesa standing in the doorway, tears streaming down her face as well. His gut twisted and he lifted one of his arms. She hurried over and stepped into the group embrace, Clare's arms growing tighter around them both. He held them close. Reesa looked up at him with a watery smile, tears clinging to her long lashes. He shifted and gently brushed a tear from her cheek, her face resting in his palm a moment before Clare pulled back to look at her mother.

"So, how'd it go?" She swiped her hands over her eyes to wipe away any remaining tears, but both stayed in the security of Theo's arms.

"Well, I'm going to have dinner with my mom and dad on Friday," Reesa announced a bit shakily. "In Hot Springs."

"You? What about me?" Clare asked.

"I want to meet with them myself first." Reesa gently brushed her fingers over Clare's cheek and smiled. "Just to see how it goes."

"Did he seem... nice?" Clare asked.

"Well... it was a bit off. He sounded older, which I guess makes sense, but it was kind of odd to hear. But he was kind, a bit stunned, and yet very to the point like he always was."

"And you?" Theo asked. "How are you?"

She snuggled herself back into his side and tugged Clare closer. "I'm alright, I think." Reesa kissed the top of Clare's head and released her. "Go inside and clean up. We'll have supper here in a bit. Check the pattern sales and comments for me, won't you?"

Clare slid out of the embrace and nodded, giving Theo a thankful nod on her way back into the cabin. Reesa's shoulders relaxed and she covered her face, holding herself together, but overwhelmed with the unfolding of the evening's events. "Reesa—" Theo grabbed her hands and slipped them down.

He didn't release them, but instead, waited until she looked at him. "I'm sad," she admitted. "I didn't know how or what I would feel if they reached out. I didn't expect it to be this soon. And I certainly didn't expect my dad to call. I had all these weird emotions just slam into me all at once." His thumbs gently massaged light circles over her knuckles as she continued. "I felt the sting of them leaving me and wanted to scream at him. But then I felt so elated that he called I wanted to blubber and cheer that I was ready to see them. And then I was angry again and trying not to sound like it. It was a roller coaster in like five minutes of stilted conversation. And now I feel completely wiped. Adrenaline dump, I guess. And I just want to snuggle up under a big blanket on my couch and zone out and watch Survivor reruns. Maybe have some wine and—"

"Hey, guys!" Jamie's voice drifted through the house and Reesa's attention flew that direction. Clearly Clare's presence stopped their friend from coming out on the back porch for now.

"I'd forgotten she was coming back over." Reesa closed her eyes a moment to collect herself.

"I'll go."

"What?" Her eyes popped open. "No, Theo—"

"You don't need me here now. Jamie's here and she will love on you and cook for you and entertain you. Before you know it, you'll be back to having a fun girl's night. You don't need me messing that up."

"You wouldn't." Reesa's eyes pleaded and he gently cupped her face in his hand again.

"I don't like seeing you cry, Reesa. I don't like seeing Clare cry either. Jamie will want the scoop, which will then lead to more tears, and I'm still soaked from the first round." He motioned to his shirt and Reesa sniffled as she grinned.

"Your sacrifice is admirable." She tugged on the front of his shirt before resting her head against the wet spot and hugging him. Without hesitancy, he wrapped his arms around her and rested his chin on the top of her head. He grunted in acknowledgement and felt her smile against him. "Thanks for being here, Theo. I hold your oath fulfilled."

"That's a movie quote, isn't it?" he mumbled.

"We're going to force you to watch Lord of the Rings at some point, my friend. It's happening." Reesa squeezed him one last time and then released. "Now go, before I change my mind and beg you to stay for supper... again." She slipped from his arms but held his hands in hers.

"You didn't beg the first time."

"Oh, I did." She batted her eyes at him. "I just didn't verbalize it." She grinned as he rolled his eyes. "And you were sweet to stay. Thank you. You were here to offer Clare support and then me support—" Reesa's voice caught in her throat, and she took a deep breath. "I'm not crying again," she stated, and though her lip quivered, she held herself together. "But thanks." Her last words were a restrained whisper as she fought her emotions. "Now go, before I hug you again."

Theo released his hold on her fingers. "Right. We can't have that." He smirked and rubbed a hand over his chin. "I'll see you. If you need anything, let me know."

"I will."

He walked around the outside of the house to avoid more disruption to the household inside. Jamie would see to the girls for the rest of the evening. There was no doubt his friend would leave them in good spirits. He reached his truck, the evening air cooling the temperature to a comfortable level that made him look forward to walking his garden and seeing Trooper before the potential rain decided to drop. However, part of him was still longing to be in the small cabin with Reesa. He was still trying to come to terms with the growing attraction he felt towards her. And he still wasn't sure if that was even worth pursuing. But being the person Clare cried on and the person Reesa sought for comfort made him stand a bit straighter. And he knew he'd protect them from anything and anyone, even Reesa's parents, if need be. His heart was compromised by the Tate women living in his grandmother's cabin. He felt it. He just had to see what that meant.

CHAPTER TWELVE

Reesa folded up her umbrella and shook the excess rain out of its panels before walking into Java Jamie. She leaned it against the wall just inside the door as her good friend popped her head out of the open archway leading to the back room where she baked her delicious treats. "Hey!" Jamie called. "I'll be out in a jiffy!"

"Take your time!" Reesa called, walking up to the counter and studying the menu she already had memorized. She indulged by taking several deep therapeutic breaths and letting the smell of Jamie's bewitching brew soothe her frazzled nerves.

A loud clap of thunder boomed, shaking the front windows as Jamie walked into her workspace. She pointed a finger up to the heavens.

"Thanks for the introduction," she giggled and continued her way towards Reesa. "Hey! What brings you out in this weather, girl?"

"Obviously your coffee." Reesa pointed to the menu and then the bags under her eyes. "And my lack of sleep."

"Still nervous about your dinner tonight with your parents?"

"Yes. Though nervous isn't exactly the word I would choose. More like terrified. And it's been a couple of days and I haven't gotten to talk to Theo about it, and I'm stressing."

"T.J. been busy?"

"Seems to be. Truth be told, I think Clare and I scared him off a bit with our sobbing the other day. He was a good sport, super supportive and caring, but I'm pretty sure we freaked him out with all the emotions just bursting forth."

"Oh, T.J. is tougher than that. He's probably just swamped at the garage."

Unconvinced, and regrettably so, Reesa shrugged. "What if we did scare him off?"

"You didn't," Jamie reassured her and then pointed to the menu. "Now, no crazy talk. What do you want this morning so we can clear the obvious cobwebs in your brain?"

"The usual." Reesa pointed to a croissant. "And one of those."

Jamie beamed and then paused. "Can we just take a moment and appreciate the fact you have now been in Piney long enough to have 'a usual'?" She punched her arm up and down and hooted like a horn of triumph before waving away her own hilarity and making Reesa's coffee.

Reesa's heart warmed at the thought of having 'a usual' as well. She'd never considered that a novelty in her life, but it truly was. She would frequent coffee shops wherever she lived, but she'd never grown so close to an owner or a place as she had with Jamie's. She felt connected to Piney already, deeply so. And when she thought of Jamie, Billy Lou, and Theo, her heart lurched at the idea of ever leaving them. They'd woven their way around her heart in such a short time that it was impossible to ignore that this was the right place for she and Clare at the right time. They were supposed to be here. She knew it. So, the dinner with her parents *had* to go well. She didn't see herself sticking around the area if it didn't. Why live so close to them if there was no point in a relationship? The whole point of moving to Piney hinged upon the fate of this dinner. Otherwise, Reesa and Clare would bust out the old map, throw a dart, and see where they'd be headed next. Sadness seeped into her already cloudy mood at the thought of uprooting Clare from the cabin. They'd found their small slice of heaven out there. A haven. A wonderful fixer-upper that gave them peace and quiet and a safe place to be their weird little selves. She loved it. Clare loved it. She didn't want to leave.

"Here you go." Jamie slid a cup across the counter with the croissant in a bag.

"I was planning on eating this here." Reesa pointed to the to-go bag and Jamie shook her head. "I'm not?" Reesa asked curiously.

"No. You're going to talk to T.J. I put two croissants in the bag and here," She slid another cup on the counter. "Another coffee. You need to see him."

"I'm not sure if *need* is the word I would use," Reesa mumbled, gathering up her load.

"Well, then, *he* needs to see *you*. Doesn't matter which way you look at it. You two need to see each other to put yourselves back to sorts."

"What?" Reesa's brows rose. "He's been in here today?"

Jamie giggled. "First thing this morning, and he looks as miserable as you do."

"Why?"

"Because he hasn't seen you," Jamie finished. "Duh."

"He said that?"

"No." Jamie scrunched her nose as she said it. "But he didn't have to. He sort of implied it." Reesa, doubtful, sighed and shook her head, placing the bag and cups back on the counter. "No, no, no. Really, he did."

"And how did he imply it?" Reesa asked.

"He mentioned he hadn't talked to you or seen you. He said Clare had been on edge the last couple of days because of tonight's dinner, and he hadn't had the time to check on you. I could tell that was eating at him. So, it will do you both good to walk your cute tooshie down the street, surprise him with a hot coffee on this gloomy day, and aggravate him like you love to do, then be on your way. You'll both feel better for it."

Reesa couldn't help the smile that blossomed over her face. "I do love to aggravate him."

"I know you do." Jamie snickered. "And he secretly likes it, I think, otherwise he wouldn't tolerate it."

Reesa grabbed the bag of croissants and coffees. "You've talked me into it. But if it goes sour, I'm coming back and demanding a refund."

"Deal." Jamie waved her out and pointed to her umbrella so she wouldn't forget it. Like she could, Reesa thought, as the rain pounded down upon her and the sidewalk. She slushed her way through the storm towards Theo's auto garage, pausing at the crosswalk and counting the seconds until the light changed. She then hurried as fast as she could, balancing the two cups and sack of breakfast, her foot landing on the opposite curb just as the light shifted again. It wasn't hard to navigate her way to Theo, but she found her steps slowing as the lights of his garage came into view. She was drenched now from the heavy downpour and the wind that decided to undercut the point of an umbrella, and her hair lay plastered to her cheeks. She blinked against the drops that pelted her face and hurried towards the glass door of the shop. She pulled it open and stepped inside, her sneakers squeaking and squishing on the tiles.

"Be right with you!" Theo's voice called from the back storage area where he could be found amongst parts and filters. He walked out carrying two small boxes and paused at the sight of her. She was sure she looked as scary and dreadful as she felt. "You're wet."

"Well," she began, shifting her accent to an overly southern drawl. "I've 'been through every kind of rain there is. Little bitty stingin' rain... and big ol' fat rain. Rain that flew in sideways. And sometimes' rain—"

"Forrest Gump," Theo stated. "Now, why are you traipsing through the rain, Reesa?"

She liked that he'd immediately picked up on her movie reference. He was getting better at doing so, and she was impressed that he'd guessed correctly to boot. "I brought you coffee. Jamie insisted you needed it."

He grunted and went about walking the two boxes out into the garage area and handing them off to Mike before coming back into the office. It was cleaner, more organized, and she could just smell the light touch of candy apple, which was Clare's favorite air freshener. Her daughter had been working hard. Theo motioned towards the bag in her hands, and she held it towards him. "A croissant." When he took it, she watched as he walked towards his desk chair, not completely ignoring her, but not offering any more conversation. She couldn't tell if he was in a cranky mood or not. "Do you like rain?" she asked, curiously.

"Doesn't everybody?" He sat in his chair and pointed to the one across from his desk. "You stayin'?"

She sat. "I feel like I haven't seen you in a while."

"You haven't."

"Well, thank you, Captain Obvious. Is there a reason why?"

He motioned to the room they sat in. "Been working. How's the deck going?"

"The rain has sort of put a hold on the work for today. Jason was out yesterday with a crew to get some of the framing up. I am now at the point of just watching and listening when he offers some sort of explanation. Not exactly what I had planned, but Billy Lou seems happy with it, and that's all that matters."

"What were you wanting to happen? To do it all yourself?"

"Essentially, yes. I wanted to get my hands dirty, have a project."

"Talk to Billy Lou. She won't be upset."

"Well, it would move slower if I did it. That's a downside. And it would be nice to see it move along at a decent pace." She trailed off at his flippant attitude. She could tell he was only half listening. She'd been thinking of him a lot the last few days. Okay, more than a lot. She'd been thinking about him constantly. And whether or not he'd been thinking of her didn't matter right now because she'd just walked through a storm to bring him coffee and a warm croissant. He was going to pay attention to her. And, she realized, she wanted more than a conversation from him. Theo took a sip of his coffee and Reesa hopped to her feet and walked around his desk, standing over him. He looked up at her, his eyes swimming with confusion. She fisted her hands on her hips. "I need you to stand up."

"Why?"

"Theo, for goodness' sake, just do it, please." She nervously fanned her hands by her side, and he set his coffee down.

"Alright, alright, calm down." He stood, "What's going on? What's wrong with y—"

Reesa jumped at him, wrapping her arms around his neck, and planting a firm kiss against his lips. They tasted of his coffee, and she felt him stiffen beneath her. She pulled her lips away from his and stared at him. "I just… I *needed* to see you." Her eyes searched his face for any sign of reciprocation, emotion, anger, elation… anything, but Theo stood frozen to the spot. She cleared her throat, and slid to her feet, her arms unwinding from around his neck. "So yeah... umm... I'm going now." Reesa reached for her purse, Theo snatching her hand before she could grasp it.

He spun her back around to face him. "Explain."

Her heart kicked into high gear, and she felt the pounding in her ears. Nervous, frantic panic welled inside her chest as she stared into his dark eyes; eyes she could stare at and melt into forever, if she allowed herself. She'd felt a growing attraction for Theo since the moment she met him. She'd depended on him in ways she'd never depended on anyone. And she liked him. Well... that was still debatable. She'd been contemplating if there was more to it than that. But she felt the buzz in the air between them. It'd been there in the beginning, and at the moment, it had turned to a sizzling undercurrent that threatened to mimic the electrical storm outside. "I don't want to right now," Reesa admitted, stepping closer to him and tilting her face up to his. She placed her hands on his chest and felt the erratic rhythm of his heart despite his outward calm. Her lips tilted in a satisfied smirk at that. He could hide it all he wanted, but he was attracted to her too. "I needed to see you." She watched as a muscle twitched in his jaw and she gently placed a kiss there. His grip tightened on her hand before sliding up to her elbow and holding her in place.

"Reesa..." His voice was barely audible. "This is not the time or place for this. I can't do this here."

"I know. I'm sorry." She leaned her forehead against his chest and felt his hand rub the back of her neck beneath her hair, the first sign of tenderness.

Growling in frustration, Theo gently tugged her head back and planted hard lips on hers. His touch softened quickly as they both melted against one another and let their feelings steer them both in new directions. His hands were in her wet hair, smoothing it away from her face as he pushed the kiss deeper. She dragged his shirt towards her, her fingers twisting into the fabric to hold him as close to her as possible. Her back bumped into the filing cabinet, and he grunted at the annoying interruption before pushing her away at the sound of the garage door opening and someone stepping inside. Mike stood in complete shock with an amused smirk on his face at catching his boss in such a situation. Reesa's heart galloped in her chest as she rested her back against the wall and watched as Theo, frazzled and embarrassed, hurried to help Mike with what he needed while trying to remain professional. When Mike walked back into the garage, Theo stood with his back to her, rubbing a hand over the back of his neck. "I told you this wasn't the place." His words held zero sting, which surprised her. When he turned, his eyes danced and he bit back a smile, rubbing a hand over his face. "This is not good."

"I'm sorry." Reesa hurried towards her purse. "I shouldn't have bombarded you like that. I just—" His hands swooped around her waist and pulled her towards him, spinning her in his arms until she crashed into his chest. He kissed her slowly, tenderly, and thoroughly until she felt as if she'd melt into a gooey puddle on the floor at his feet. Satisfied, Theo stepped away from her. "I'll be over after work, and we can discuss this." He nudged her towards the door. "But you need to leave. *Now.*" She'd never seen his eyes so captivating and stared at him in wonder. "Reesa, seriously." His hands nervously grabbed her purse and handed it to her. "Go. I'll see you later, okay? We'll talk about this. But I need to process this, and I can't with you here. I just... can't." Desire flamed, and she nodded, stunned by the heat and magnetism that exploded between them. "Reesa," he said again, his voice gruff.

"Okay," She snapped to attention. "I'm going. I'm just distracted and completely in awe of this side of you. I- I like it."

His face flushed and she reached up to touch his cheek. He grabbed her hand and brought it down to her side, tugging her towards him for one last toe-curling kiss that had her knees knocking and clumsily walking up the street towards Jamie's. She turned, the rain showering down on her head, and saw him standing in front of his shop, eyes focused only on her. She wanted to go back to him. She wanted to be swept up into his strong arms and breathtaking kisses. Had she known how powerfully captivating he was? Had she known that giving in to a harmless kiss would result in this? In this beautiful feeling of completeness? Did she just fall in love with Theodore Whitley of Piney, Arkansas? She stared at him a moment longer and kissed the tips of her fingers and waved. Yes, she admitted, she had. Deep down she knew her heart had just leapt from her chest and merged with his. And now— the connection, the heat, the passion, the love— all of the things she'd ever wanted could be hers. If she allowed them to be.

~

Clare eyed him over the top of a parts catalog, watching his every move, only talking when asked a question, not jabbering away about her school day like she normally did. He missed her chatter. He hadn't realized he'd gotten used to it. But he was curious as to her latest shenanigans— whether Teddy Graham was still dating the girl who didn't like Clare, or whether or not the football team was ready for Friday night's game— questions that he wouldn't dare ask, but knew were at the forefront of Clare's day to day. Instead, she studied him, scrutinizing his every move until he couldn't handle it anymore. "Is there something wrong, Clare?" he asked, fisting his hands on his hips. "You've been quiet and beady-eyed all afternoon."

"I don't have beady eyes." She gawked in horror at the suggestion but set the catalog on his desk. "I'm just waiting for you to tell me."

"Tell you what?" Theo asked.

"About kissing my mom."

His jaw momentarily dropped before he composed himself, though he could feel the heat climbing up his neck and to his cheeks. "Who told you that?"

"Mike. He said he caught you 'neckin' with my 'hot mom.' Which, by the way, is weird to hear any way, especially from Mike. But 'neckin' only means one thing, right? Kissing? So, is it true? Did you kiss my mom?"

Theo, feeling trapped, didn't like this sort of conversation. In fact, he avoided them as much as possible. But Clare deserved to know the truth. Besides, she was part of the picture. If he did pursue Reesa, that meant he pursued a relationship with Clare as well. Obviously, a different kind of relationship, but a relationship nonetheless, and she deserved to have input. "I did."

He waited, curious as to the thoughts running around her head until she let out an excited squeal and jumped to her feet. She danced her way over to him and hugged him tight around the middle. "I knew it! I knew it! I knew it!" She beamed up at him. "Okay, tell me how it happened. Tell me everything." She hurried back over to the desk and popped the tab on a fresh soda, propping her feet up on his desk. "Don't leave out any details."

His right brow lifted, and she paused on her first sip. "Oh." Disappointment settled upon her face as she lowered her feet. "Right. I forgot. You're a boy. Boys don't dissect things like girls do, and you certainly don't share every little detail." She took a suffering sip of her soda. "Guess I'll have to wait and hear about it from Mom. Though she probably won't be in a talkative mood because this dinner with her parents has her completely stressed out." Her eyes narrowed at him. "You didn't take advantage of her being distracted, did you? You didn't kiss her because she was in a vulnerable emotional state, did you?" Her voice hardened and he shook his head.

"No." He growled when he saw she didn't believe him. "No," he said again. "I wouldn't do that. Besides, she came in here and kissed me. So, yeah, turn that question around on her next time you see her." He awkwardly walked away and into the parts room, Clare hot on his heels.

"Mom kissed *you*? Seriously?" She giggled. "Way to go, Mom."

Theo paused, his face showing his interest in her last comment.

"It's just Mom normally doesn't really do that. You know, make the first move. She must really like you. I mean, I knew she did, I just didn't realize how much."

"You knew she had feelings for me? Why didn't you say anything?"

Clare rolled her eyes. "Because she didn't really tell me, tell me. I just *knew*. Kind of like I know you have feelings for her. You two have been tiptoeing around one another since day one. It's been kind of fun to watch, though."

"Great." Theo's dry response had her happily drumming her hands on his arm.

"Don't be such a fuddy duddy. This is exciting." Clare smiled. "I mean, I think it is. Do you?"

"Not sure if 'exciting' is the word I would use," Theo admitted, reaching up to the top of a shelf and removing a three-ring binder with product codes listed inside. "New, different," Theo continued. "That's how I'd explain it."

"And exciting," Clare finished for him. "Because you can't tell me you haven't been thinking about her all day, right?"

Theo shot her a quick glance and she squealed. He bit back a grin as he brushed past her back into the office, Clare hovering behind him. He tried to concentrate on the numbers in the binder, but Clare continued to stare at him. He closed the binder on a sigh and looked at her. "Clare?"

"Hm?" she asked, eager to do whatever he asked. Her joy over the situation pleased him, but he also felt awkward with her gawking.

"Shouldn't you be at the desk?"

"Oh, right." She snapped her fingers and hurried around him to her spot just as the phone on the desk rang. She answered with a chipper tone and then covered the receiver. "It's my mom asking if you'll marry her."

His face blanched and she laughed. "Kidding! It's Mr. Helms wondering when he can come get his truck."

Not amused, Theo snatched the phone from her hand and talked with his customer. When he hung up, he turned to find Clare beaming at him. "Okay, clearly we need to set some things straight." Her face immediately fell, and her eyes grew sad.

"What are you doing?" he asked. "Why are you looking at me like that?"

"This is where you tell me that it was a mistake to kiss my mom. That you're better off friends. That you shouldn't have crossed that line. Blah, blah, blah. I've heard all this before. Just get it over with." Clare waved him onward, and he shook his head.

"No. I wasn't going to say any of that. I was just going to say that I don't want any teasing about this. It's between your mom and me right now. We haven't even gotten to discuss it yet. For all I know, she could think it a big mistake. So, until we talk about it, I don't want to..." He searched for the right way to explain when Clare interrupted.

"You don't want to get my hopes up?" Clare asked. She stood and hugged him tight around the waist.

"Again with the hugging?" he asked and felt her laugh.

"Yes. It's what we do. And you're a good person, Theo. And for what it's worth, I hope this really does become something between you and my Mom, but, if nothing does come of it, I'll be cool, and I hope you will be too."

Theo nodded and she released him. "I'm going out in the shop now." He pointed over her shoulder, and she stepped out of his way. He'd finish Mr. Helms' oil change and then he'd take Clare home. It wouldn't be weird, he told himself. When he saw Reesa again, he'd keep his hands to himself. They'd talk with a comfortable two feet, no... four feet between them, so as not to muddle what was being said. They both needed to take a step back and evaluate what had happened and what they wanted moving forward. Perhaps it was a momentary lapse in judgment on her part and she let the stress of tonight's dinner cloud that judgment. But what if it was genuine? What transpired between them had been good. *Real* good. He hadn't felt this way about anyone that he could remember. All he wanted was to be near Reesa, hear her laugh, watch her smooth her hair behind her ear, watch her work on whatever yarn project she had stored away in that fascinating and quirky brain of hers. He wanted to touch her, hold her, kiss her, and to his surprise, love her. He wanted to protect her. And Clare. He'd recently figured out that Clare had wriggled her way into his heart as well when she'd come in from school upset about Teddy's girlfriend still causing trouble. The boy would get a clue, he knew, but Theo did not like to see Clare suffer in any shape or form. And if Reesa's parents rejected them both, he was ready to fight to keep them in Piney. He knew Reesa's instinct would be to run to a new place. But he was not about to let that happen. Not now. Not now that he'd lost his heart to her. He twisted the drain plug in place and then added the new filter to Mr. Helms' truck. He grabbed the undertray and attached it, sliding out from under the truck. He lowered the jack and the truck rested back on its wheels. He popped the hood and removed the oil cap, filling the engine with the specified oil. He checked the dipstick twice to make sure the levels were okay and then screwed the cap back in place. He closed the hood, rubbed his greasy hands on a towel and walked back into the office. Clare glanced up. "Ready to go?"

"Yep." She nodded out the door at Mr. Helms talking with Mike. "I already checked him out. His keys in the truck?"

"Yes." Theo walked over to the sink and began washing his hands as Clare walked outside to report to Mr. Helms that he could now take his truck home. The older gentleman nodded with a smile and handed Clare some cash. She thanked him and walked inside.

"He tipped me." She grinned. "Am I able to keep this? Or is there a tip jar?"

Theo smirked. "It's yours. We don't usually get tips, so any tips you keep."
"Awesome." Clare pocketed the cash and then glanced at her cell phone. "It's six."

"Yeah, I'll get you home. Your Mom is probably wondering why it's taken us so long."

"She's in Hot Springs by now." Clare nibbled her bottom lip, the action a mirror of her mother.

"Right." Theo sighed. "I should have had you home before she left."

"No, this is for the best. She was probably a frazzled mess and wouldn't want me to see her that way. But I would not turn down a trip by the burger joint on the way home so I can grab some supper. I'm really tired of toaster pastries right now."

"I'll do you one better." Theo walked towards his truck and Clare hopped in the passenger side. "We'll go bug Billy Lou for supper."

"She won't mind?"

"Nope." He motioned ahead of them on the street at Jamie's coffee shop. "Is that Teddy there?"

"Yep." Clare shifted. "What are you doing?"

Theo slowed down and pulled up next to the curb and rolled down his window. "Hey, Teddy. How's it going?"

The young man glanced up, his smile brightening at seeing Clare. "Hey."

"We're headed to Billy Lou's for supper. Want to join?" Theo asked.

Teddy glanced at his phone and back at Jamie's. "Let me text my parents to let them know. But sure, that'd be fun. I haven't seen Ms. Billy Lou in a while."

Theo looked to the cars parked along the curb. "You have wheels?"

"No sir. I hitched a ride with friends."

"Well, hop in. You can scoot over, right Clare?" Theo thumbed over his shoulder to the passenger side and Clare, eyes wide at what was happening, scooted to the middle of the seat to let Teddy slide in. When Teddy had shut the door, Theo headed towards his grandmother's house.

"How have you been, Clare?" Teddy asked.

Theo felt Clare stiffen next to him as she tried to appear nonchalant. "Good. You?"

The boy shrugged. "Been busy working on my English essay. You finish yours yet?"

She nodded. "Yesterday."

"Lucky." Teddy grinned. "You going to the dance next Friday?"

"Not sure yet." Clare's fingers fumbled with the zipper on her backpack. "You?"

"I think so. Not really sure."

"Is it lame? Is that why you don't want to go?" Clare asked.

"No, it's usually pretty fun. It was last year, anyway," Teddy explained.

"Then why wouldn't you go this year?"

A slight awkwardness filled the truck and Theo bit back a smile as he turned down the driveway to his grandmother's house. Billy Lou stepped outside, her face brightening at the sight of company. She waved a manicured hand in their direction as Theo pulled to a stop. Teddy hopped out, holding the truck door for Clare as she slid to the ground. "Thanks." She walked past him into Billy Lou's open embrace.

"My, my, my! Did I just win the lottery?" Billy Lou asked, giving Teddy a hug as well.

"We come begging for a meal, Grandma," Theo stated. "Reesa's in Hot Springs, Clare and Teddy are starving, and I am just too lazy to cook tonight."

"Well, I couldn't ask for better guests. Come on in." She bustled inside leading the way to the grand kitchen she'd remodeled not long after her husband's death. It had been the first project to lose herself to avoid the grief she felt. She'd since come to terms with the loss, though Theo knew she missed cooking for more than just herself. "I was thinkin' of making some meatloaf. Does that sound alright?"

"That sounds amazing." Teddy's phone dinged with a text message, and he glanced down, a slight frown etching his forehead.

"You okay?" Clare asked in a soft whisper to avoid interference from the grownups.

"Just Gracie."

Theo assumed that was the girlfriend that disliked Clare.

"Everything okay?" Clare asked.

He shook his head. "We broke up this afternoon."

"Oh." Clare, though Theo knew she didn't like the girl, gave Teddy an encouraging pat. "I'm sorry to hear that."

The teen shrugged. "It's for the best. She was too... I don't know, possessive. I couldn't hang out with anyone anymore. You and Tyler mostly."

"Why not Tyler? He's your best friend."

"She just didn't like him."

"Weird." Teddy smirked at her reply, and she quickly tried to explain. "I mean—"

"It's cool," Teddy assured her. "It was weird."

"I guess that's why you may not go to the dance?" Clare asked.

"Yep." Teddy leaned back in his chair at the small dinette table as Billy Lou brought Theo a cutting board and set one up right next to him so they could both eavesdrop. She handed him an onion and they both began chopping quietly to hear the conversation in front of them. Teddy looked at Clare and smirked. "Unless you want to go with me."

She flushed and avoided her friend's gaze but caught Theo's eye. Theo winked at her and she blushed even further. Her back straightened a bit. "Is this you asking me because you want me to be your date? Or is this you just wanting to have someone to make Gracie mad? Because yes to the first, no to the second." Clare's adamant response had Teddy studying her a moment, slightly taken aback by her answer.

He then leaned towards her and nervously took her hand in his. "Clare, would you be my date to the dance next Friday? Not because I want to be mean towards Gracie, but because you're my friend and I've missed spending time with you."

Clare flashed a quick look to Billy Lou who gave her an encouraging nod. "Sure. Sounds like fun."

Relief washed over Teddy's face as he smiled. "Cool."

Theo's phone buzzed in his pocket, and he saw Reesa's name light up the screen. "It's your mom." He swiped his finger over the phone and held it to his ear. Before he could greet her, Reesa's panicked voice flooded the line. "I don't know if I can do this. I think I'm going to vomit. I'm scared. I'm furious. I'm wearing a dress."

"Deep breaths." Theo stepped away from the counter and walked outside to stand on the back deck and watched the trees blow in the wind. Reesa inhaled and exhaled slowly into the phone. "Are you in the restaurant?"

"No. Not yet. I'm in the car waiting in the valet line."

"Valet?"

"Yes, leave it to my parents to choose one of the fanciest restaurants in the city. Which I feel supremely underdressed for, mind you, because I hardly own any dresses anymore." Reesa's nerves fluttered over the line.

"Deep breath again," Theo told her. "I'm sure you look great. Besides, I don't think they'll care what you're wearing."

"You don't know my mother," Reesa mumbled.

"And neither do you," Theo pointed out. "It's been almost sixteen years, Reesa. She may be different than you remember."

"That's true." Her tone shifted to a more positive outlook. "Thank you. Look at me only thinking of the negative and being dramatic. Fifteen years is a long time. People change. I'm proof of that. Yes, I should give her the benefit of the doubt. How was Clare today?"

Theo glanced over his shoulder and peered through the windows, Clare and Teddy had heads bent over Billy Lou's current puzzle on the end of the bar while his grandmother cooked. "She's good. I brought her to Billy Lou's for supper. Teddy's with us."

"Oh, that's an interesting turn of events."

"Apparently he and his girlfriend broke up."

"Oooooh…" Reesa's voice held curiosity. "Can't wait to hear more about that. Eyes and ears, Theo. You're my eyes and ears."

He chuckled. "I'll do my best."

"Oh shoot, it's my turn."

He heard the greeting, the shifting, the door closing, and then Reesa came back on the line. "Okay, I'm walking inside now."

"You've got this."

"Do I?" Reesa cleared her throat. "Oh geez, I can't cry yet. I have to save that for afterwards. This is where I could really use… well, you. Why didn't you come with me? Why didn't I ask? Then we could both feel awkward and scared and completely not at ease together. That'd be easier, wouldn't it? Or Jamie. Why didn't I bring Jamie? She's good at breaking the ice. How do you break fifteen-year-old ice?"

"Reesa, you're spiraling. Calm down and take a deep breath. You're not alone. At any point you can call me, okay?" A long silence. "Reesa?"

"I see them." Her whisper was barely audible. "Oh, Theo." Her voice cracked. "I see them."

"Listen to me, Reesa. You listening?"

"I'm listening." Her quiet voice held such hurt, his heart ached for her.

"You're beautiful. Inside and out, you're beautiful. You're the most welcoming, imposing, weird, gorgeous woman I've ever met. You're special. And geez, you have an incredible kid. You've done an amazing job with Clare. No matter how tonight goes, you just remember all of that, okay? You're the most beautiful person I've ever met." He waited a second. "Reesa?"

"Yeah, so I'm crying again. Thanks for that." She sniffled. "Thanks, Theo. I'm going to call you when I leave here."

"I'll do better than that. I'll wait for you at your place."

"I don't know how late I'll be."

"I don't care. I'll wait." A protectiveness seeped out in his tone, and he heard her sniff back tears.

"You're a good man, Theodore Whitley. I'll see you in a little while."

"Deep breath." He hung up and turned to find Billy Lou standing on the porch behind him, the two kids inside the house.

Her eyes held unshed tears as she stared at him. "You love her?" she asked.

He stared at her a moment and then nodded.

"Good." Billy Lou nodded back in approval and stretched out her arm for him to walk into the house with her. "Supper's ready."

CHAPTER THIRTEEN

Reesa watched as the waiter sat her parents at a white cloth table, her mother impeccably dressed in a black, slim-fitting dress, her hair perfectly curled at the tips. She'd barely aged, Reesa thought, with only a few grays peeking through the dark hair. Her dad looked older, more tired than she remembered, but he was still tall and dressed in an expensively cut suit which she knew would smell like spicy aftershave. She glanced in the front window to check her reflection and sniffed back her emotions and squared her shoulders. She was smart, beautiful, successful, and loved whether they accepted her or not, she was loved by others, by Clare, and that was enough. She walked to the hostess and mentioned her name, the woman smiling and handing her off to one of the waiters who escorted her towards the table. Her heart hammered in her chest as she approached the table. Her mother glanced up first, startled, and then her dad turned around. He stood, his eyes soaking in every inch of her. "Dad." She took the offered chair from the waiter and slid in between her parents, setting her purse under the table.

Her dad sat, his eyes never leaving her face, his hand gently touching the top of hers and giving it a small pat. "Reesa."

"Mom." She offered a smile at her mother, but her mother avoided her gaze and took a sip of her complimentary water instead. Reesa felt the burn of resentment but stifled it down to try and stay positive. "Thank you both for meeting with me."

"Of course." Roger Tate motioned towards the waiter. "How about we all order our drinks and maybe an appetizer." The waiter stepped up and Roger ordered for himself and his wife and then turned to Reesa to see what she would like.

"Just a tea for me, thanks." The waiter penciled on his notepad and hurried away.

"You didn't bring your child?" her father asked.

"I thought it best that it just be me this first time," Reesa admitted, hoping they respected her decision and realized they didn't even know if she'd had a baby boy or a baby girl. The thought saddened her more.

"We've never met the child, why would she let us now?" Her mother's bitter tone sliced through the air and Roger narrowed his gaze on his wife to rein in her emotions.

"Yes, well, I'm protective of Clare, my *daughter.*" Reesa shrugged as if that was just how it was. And it honestly was.

"As if she'd need protection from her own grandparents, honestly." Her mother took another sip of her water until the waiter walked up with her glass of wine and she took a long and generous sip of it.

"So," Her dad ignored his wife and looked at Reesa. "You and your daughter live in Hot Springs?"

Reesa shook her head. "No. I live over in Piney."

"Oh, there's great hiking over that direction. I hear the pine forests and mountains are gorgeous. We haven't ventured over to Piney in years."

Reesa appreciated her father's attempts at small talk as she dodged the darts from her mother's angry gaze. "We like it so far," Reesa admitted. "The people are extremely kind."

"And what do you do in Piney?" he asked.

"I work from home," Reesa explained. "I create crochet patterns and have an online store and teach online classes."

Her father nodded, though she could tell he didn't quite understand anything about it. "How have you two been?" Reesa asked.

"Oh," Her dad motioned toward her mother. "We've been traveling more now that I'm retired. We'd just gotten back from Paris when we received your letter."

"Paris?" Reesa asked. "Wow. That sounds exciting."

"It was lovely. Virginia has always wanted to go, and we finally made it happen."

"That's wonderful." Reesa took a sip of her tea and heard her cell phone buzz against the side of her purse. "I'm sorry," She reached down and retrieved it. "I need to make sure this isn't Clare. She's at a friend's house this evening." She glanced down and saw Theo's name, peace washing over her at the picture he sent of Teddy, Clare, and Billy Lou laughing over supper. Yes, she had a wonderful group of people waiting for her in Piney. And she loved him even more for knowing that's what she'd need at this very moment during her own awkward supper.

"Everything okay?" her father asked.

"Yes." She smiled and put her phone away. "She's doing great."

"Can we see some pictures of her?" her father shyly asked.

Reesa's heart flipped and she nodded. "Of course. I'm sorry I didn't think of that." She pulled her phone back out and scanned through her photos until she reached a few flattering photos of Clare and handed it to him. Her dad held a hand to his heart and leaned back in his chair, his eyes filling with tears. "My word, she's beautiful. Virginia, take a look." He turned the phone towards his wife, her mother feigning indifference, though her eyes soaked in the images he flipped through. "Absolutely beautiful." With a watery smile, he handed the phone back to Reesa. "And who is the gentleman next to her?"

Reesa looked down at the last photo and realized he'd swiped one photo too far and saw a photo of Theo and Clare in Theo's garden. "That's our neighbor, Theo. He's been teaching Clare about gardening."

"That's wonderful. And how does she like school?"

"She loves it. She makes friends easily and seems to enjoy Piney so far."

"And you've been in Piney how long?"

"Almost four weeks."

"Oh, so the move has been recent," Roger added.

"Yes." Reesa felt her mother staring at her.

"So, you've been within thirty miles of us for less than a month and you're already reaching out. What do you need from us?" her mother quipped.

"Virginia—" Roger scolded under his breath.

"Come now, Roger, she clearly needs something. Why else would she be contacting us after all this time? Need money for her college? Is that it? A car? What?"

Reesa leaned back against her chair and let the insults come her way. Her mother was hurt, understandably so, but so was she. When her mother had finished her rant, Reesa looked her mother in the eye. "We don't need anything from you. We have a happy, peaceful, wonderful life together." She looked at her dad who seemed to be the most open-minded of the two of them. "I was watching her the other day and realized I'd been selfish with her. She's beautiful, kind, smart, funny... and for a brief second my selfishness at keeping her to myself became apparent and I thought I might be doing her a disservice by not letting her know you two, and vice versa. I thought I would try to reach out for that reason, and that reason only. I also understand if you do not want to meet her or get to know her. We are prepared for that scenario as well."

"Lord in Heaven, you told her we wouldn't want to meet her?" Her mother's aghast response had the neighboring table glancing over.

"No, Mom, I didn't. I just wasn't sure if... well, if I'd be welcome in your life after all this time. It has nothing to do with her, and she knows that."

"You've probably painted us as horrible people to her," Virginia continued. "After all, what kind of mother would leave her daughter at a pregnancy clinic and just walk away, right? Never mind the fact we thought it the best option at the time."

Reesa disagreed but kept her own opinion and feelings to herself. She didn't want to fight, especially in a public place. And this might be the only conversation she'd ever have with her parents. She wanted them to know she'd long since let the past go. "That's water under the bridge, Mom. I forgave you a long time ago."

"*Forgave us?*" Virginia's voice shrilled. "Did you hear that, Roger? She forgave *us*. As if the humiliation of having a pregnant teenager wasn't tough to handle, as if her decisions did not affect this entire family. Forgiving *us* of all things. You will never understand the embarrassment and heartbreak you caused." Her mother shook her head in disgust, grabbing her clutch and standing to her feet. "Excuse me, I need to use the ladies' room." She hurried off, Reesa and her father watching her go.

A deep sigh brought Reesa's attention back to her father and he mustered a tired smile. "Your mother—"

"Hasn't really changed?" Reesa asked.

"That's not very fair, Reesa. This is a shock to us all. The hurt from so long ago and the absence of you in our lives has all been brought to the forefront this evening. It's a lot to take in. She just needs a little time to process it all."

"The absence of me?" Reesa asked. "You two left me at the clinic and never came back." She looked confused. "I waited. They let me stay there and clean the facilities for room and board an extra six months after Clare was born because they were trying to contact you to come and get me. You never did." Her voice grew quiet as she bit back a

KATHARINE E. HAMILTON

sob. "You never did." Swallowing back the lump in her throat, she continued. "After that, I moved on."

Her father rested his chin on his chest and pressed his thumbs to his eyes before reaching across the table and squeezing her hand in his. "To my everlasting shame, Reesa. I regret dropping you off at that place." He sobbed quietly in his seat. "I will never forgive myself."

She felt her own tears slip down her cheeks and leaned over to rest her head on her dad's shoulder. He crossed his arm over his chest to gently hold her head there as he rested his temple against her hair. "My darlin'," he whispered, the old pet name he'd given her when she was a toddler rolling off his tongue as smooth as it had back then.

"I forgive you, Daddy," she whispered. "I honestly do, and I'd love for you to get to know Clare. But right now, I'm going to go. I don't want to upset Mom more than she already is. You just let me know when you'd like to see us, okay?" She stood, gathering her purse on her shoulder. He collected himself and found his feet as well. Reesa stepped towards him and wrapped her arms around his waist in a hug. She slipped away quickly. "I hope to see you again." She walked away just as she saw her mother exit the ladies' room. When she stepped outside, she gasped for air and a loud sob escaped her lips, the valet giving her a look of concern. She handed him her ticket and he quickly fetched her keys and disappeared. She withdrew her phone and sent a quick text to Theo letting her know she was on her way home.

Theo: *"We'll be here waiting for you."*

A tear fell onto her phone screen, and she smiled at the hope that flooded her chest at the thought of him and Clare being in the cozy cabin when she walked in the door. The valet returned with her car, accepted the tip she gave him, and then shut her inside the safety of her vehicle. She pulled away from the curb and headed towards Piney, headed towards home.

~

Theo watched as Reesa's headlights slowly made their way up the bumpy dirt road towards the cabin. He'd been waiting, sitting on the front porch as Clare mindlessly watched a movie inside the house. Something about 'stress-eating cookies until Mom comes back,' and her hands flying with a crochet hook and yarn just like her mother. He figured by the time Reesa showed up, Clare would have an entire blanket created at the speed she was going. He wasn't used to waiting on someone, and the last hour or so had ticked by extremely slowly. But he enjoyed the woods, and the after-storm weather left the temperature cool and damp enough that the pine trees perfumed the air and the wind kept him comfortable. He rocked in the rocking chair and waited until she parked and trudged her way to the steps. She didn't see him in the dark and jumped when he said her name. Hand on her heart, relief washed over her at seeing him stand up and come towards her and into the light. "I could have sprayed you with my pepper spray again, Theo. Did you not learn your lesson the first time?"

His lips twitched before he tugged her towards him and wrapped his arms around her. She softened against him and just stood and let him hold her. "Your daughter is going to gain a hundred pounds if you do not walk in there and prove you are okay."

Reesa held on to him. "Just one more minute."

"Alright." His grip around her tightened and he rested his chin on the top of her head. "You good?"

"Not really." Her response had him rubbing warmth up and down her back with his hands before tugging her away from him so he could look into her eyes. "It was so hard," she told him, her voice weary, as she walked towards the front door. "And I want to tell you all about it, but I need to see Clare."

"I can meet you tomorrow at Jamie's."

"No. Please stay for a while. I..." She turned to face him square on. "Theo, I really need you right now, if that's okay?"

Her words pelted against his heart, and he gave a small nod. "I'm here then."

She extended her hand to him, and he laced his fingers with hers as she walked inside the door. One of the latest Star Trek movies blasted on the television as Clare's furious fingers crocheted together two giant granny squares of dark and broody colors. When the door squeaked and closed, her head snapped around, her eyes first landing on her mother's tired and tear-stained face, then their joined hands, and then back to Reesa. She turned off the television and stood, slowly setting aside the crochet project in her hands. "I take it they weren't very nice."

Sighing, Reesa walked towards Clare, dragging Theo along with her, and brought them together in a group hug which resulted in Theo being the foundation and the front of his shirt being soaked in Tate female tears once again, only this time he didn't mind at all.

"Oh, baby." Reesa brushed a hand over Clare's hair. "My daddy thought you were so beautiful. So, so, so beautiful." She smiled despite her tears and hugged Clare closer. Reesa swiped a hand over her face and cupped Clare's chin with the other. "I have a feeling he will want to meet you soon, if you want to."

"And your mom?" Clare asked.

Reesa shook her head. "I don't know. She's... hurt."

Clare's back stiffened at her words. "*She's* hurt? What could *she* possibly be hurt over? *She's* the one who—"

"Clare, honey, there's so much pain between her and I. It's not all on her. It might just take some time for her to come around. But my dad seems open to the idea of getting to know you."

"Can I think about it?" Clare asked.

"Of course." Reesa nodded. "Of course." She hugged Clare again and then glanced up at Theo. "Now, enough of this crying business. It's been a long night. I'm starving because I left before we ordered supper, so I'm going to pop in a frozen pizza and eat while you two tell me about your time at Billy Lou's. And Teddy. When did he come back into the picture?"

Clare walked to the kitchen to start preparing Reesa's pizza for her as her mother took off her raincoat and hung it to dry. Then she held up a finger. "Wait, I'm going to change first." She motioned to the dress she wore. "Because I am tired of this."

Clare snorted as if it were a ridiculous sight to see her mother wearing a dress, but Theo couldn't look away. When Reesa started to pass by him, his hand acted on its own and grasped her arm. She paused a moment and let him openly survey her appearance. The boho maxi dress clung to every curve of her body, the wild print fitting of Reesa's personality.

"Like what you see there, Theo?" Clare teased, grabbing a bag of chips off the top of the refrigerator.

Theo's eyes flashed Clare's direction a moment before he focused on Reesa again. "Mike told Clare we kissed this morning." Theo pointed a finger over Reesa's shoulder towards the happy teenager dancing in the kitchen. "I didn't deny it."

"Well, it happened," Reesa admitted, looking her daughter's direction. "How do you feel about it?"

"I'm totally okay with it." Clare grinned. "I think it aggravates Theo though."

Reesa giggled as she slipped her arm around his waist. "That's what makes it fun." She danced her fingers up his chest and to his chin, giving it a tap with her pointer finger. Her smile faltered when he looked down at her, his eyes serious. He heard her sharp intake of breath before he closed his mouth over hers once more. He heard Clare laugh in the kitchen before he relinquished Reesa and nudged her towards her bedroom. Reesa fanned her flushed face and winked at her daughter before hurrying down the hall. Theo cleared his throat, embarrassed his control had slipped in front of Clare.

"Theo, don't take this the wrong way, okay?" Clare offered him a chip. "But you're seriously the cutest dude I've ever met."

Baffled, Theo paused in pulling his hand out of the bag. "I'm not sure how to take that, Clare."

She gave him a hearty pat on the arm. "With a forced smile, like you do everything else." Giggling, she bypassed him back to the living room, the teen seemingly resilient to the day's events. He still stood in the kitchen when Reesa buzzed back into the room dressed in comfortable shorts and oversized t-shirt. She'd swept her hair into a messy bun on top of her head and walked barefoot across the floor. She paused in front of him to snag a chip. "You okay?"

He blinked, snapping himself to attention. "I'm just continually amazed at how odd you two are."

"It's a blessing in disguise," Reesa assured him. "Nothing keeps us down for long. Besides, we love each other, so we have that at the end of a very long day. Isn't that right, Clare?"

"Yep," her teen called over her shoulder as she sat on the couch with her feet tucked under her, snacking on chips.

Reesa's tender smile towards Clare was contented and he questioned whether he truly did fit in their perfectly designed pattern of a life. "So, eat with me?" Reesa asked, leading the way to the small kitchen table. "I know you two probably had a fabulous meal over at Billy Lou's, but I could eat an entire cow right now." Theo found an empty seat as she walked to the cabinet and withdrew an empty cup and then took it over to the freezer to fill it with ice. "I just need a giant glass of ice water. I think I cried all the water out of my system on the way home." She turned on the tap, filled her glass, and walked over to the table, sitting in the chair adjacent to him. "Now, tell me some good news. Tell me about Teddy," she whispered, casting a curious glance at Clare.

"Apparently the girlfriend is no longer in the picture," Theo mumbled. "And he asked Clare to a dance on Friday."

"The homecoming dance?" Reesa asked curiously.

"I have no idea."

"You didn't ask?" Reesa challenged.

"I didn't think it was my business. Besides, I didn't want to embarrass them."

"Well, I'm glad they're back to being friends. She was a bit down the last couple of weeks to have her first friend so distant. I couldn't last three days without talking to you, I can only imagine how she felt."

"First friend, hm?" Theo didn't like the sound of that after he thought they'd moved past friendship that morning.

"Yes. You were my first friend here, even if you didn't consider me your friend at the time." Reesa frowned when she saw the confusion on his face. "What is it?"

Theo leaned back against the chair and studied her. "And what am I now?" he asked. He had to know. He had to know if what they'd shared that morning and even in her own living room ten minutes prior meant more to her than friendship.

Reesa reached across the tabletop and brushed her fingers over the back of his hand. Theo turned his hand palm up and Reesa rested hers on top. "Theo, I'm... I'm not great at relationships." Reesa held up her free hand to stop his temper from rising. "This isn't me saying I don't want one." She offered a sad smile. "I'm just not great at them. I have baggage. Lots of it. And I tend to let it interfere with my emotions every now and then. I do everything I can to give Clare a good life, a happy life. The few times I've attempted relationships, they've fizzled into nothing because I can never fully trust— well, trust anyone with my daughter. I'm selfish, I guess. And I've never found someone who fully embraces me and Clare. We're a package deal, and—"

"I'm fine with that."

Reesa's eyes softened. "I can tell." A watery smile crossed her face as she squeezed his hand. "You're different, Theo. And I care about you, and I can tell you care about Clare and me."

"I do." He shifted, leaning closer to her and gently cupped her face in his free hand. "I do, more than I thought I could. In less than a month you have completely knocked me off my feet, Reesa." He shook his head on a smile. "And I will admit, I'm still getting used to it. I'm not so great at relationships either. In fact, I avoid them as best I can. But you refuse to be ignored. I tried." She snorted back a laugh and he lightly brushed his fingers up and behind her temple to tuck the silky hair away. "So, it may not be easy for either of us at first, but I'm in it. I want you to know that. I'll prove it to you, somehow, because I want this. I want you in my life."

"Even if it gets messy sometimes?"

"Especially when it's messy."

"Even if I annoy you?"

"You always annoy me." He lightly pressed his lips to hers. "I'm growing to love it." Her smile broke the kiss. "And how to do you feel about teenage emotional breakdowns?"

"She can go work it out in the garden."

"Hard labor?" Reesa tilted her head. "I never thought of that option." Giggling softly, she focused back on him and kissed the back of his hand. "I have to talk to Clare about this. See what she says."

"I already said I was cool with it, Mom!" Clare called from the couch, hanging on their every word. She grinned at Theo before turning back to her movie. He didn't even feel embarrassed that the girl was eavesdropping on their intimate conversation. It did involve her too, and he was glad he'd made an impression on Clare.

"Well, alright then." Reesa leaned towards Theo, this time she kissed the tip of his nose and brushed her fingers down his lightly bearded cheek. "On one condition."

"Let me guess, no beard?"

Biting her lip to hide a laugh, she kissed him with such heart, he surrendered to her wish. "I'll never grow it again if you keep kissing me like that."

"I came here tonight because when you realize you want to spend the rest of your life with somebody, you want the rest of your life to start as soon as possible," Reesa whispered against his lips.

"Reesa—" Theo pulled back to look down at her and narrowed his eyes.

Laughing, she called, "Clare, put on When Harry Met Sally! We need to further Theo's education." She pecked his lips, hopped to her feet, removed her pizza from the oven, taking the whole pan to the coffee table, and waved him over. Clare scooted to the corner of the cushions, her hands still working vigorously on her crochet project as Theo sat between her and Reesa.

"Alright." He looked at Reesa, a face he wished to memorize and love for the rest of his life. "Let's do this."

EPILOGUE

Reesa held up a glass of tea she'd freshly poured for Theo as he trudged up the stairs to her new deck, carrying a bucket of vegetables. She kissed his lips, never tiring of the thrill it shot through her veins. He set the bucket beside the grill, kissed her intently, then released her to accept the glass and say hello to Billy Lou and Roger Tate, who sat at the new patio table. Clare played with Trooper in the yard, tossing the tennis ball as far as it would go, the poor dog never giving up and insistent upon never-ending throws. "We couldn't get started without you," Reesa whispered, giving a slight nod her father's direction. "He came." Excitement filled her voice at her dad accepting her invitation to come visit.

"I'm glad. And Clare?"

"They've hit it off really well. Thank God for Billy Lou, though. When conversation stills, she navigates us back to something to talk about. Have I mentioned that I love her?"

"On several occasions," Theo reminded her, walking towards her dad. Roger stood to his feet and extended his hand. "Theodore Whitley," Theo introduced.

"Roger Tate." Reesa's dad looked down at Theo's other hand holding Reesa's and then gave an affirmative nod. "Nice to meet you. I've heard much about you."

"That so?" Theo looked down at Reesa and smiled.

"From Clare," Roger finished and had Reesa snickering at Theo's blunder.

"Ah. Well, that could go either way, couldn't it?" Theo laughed.

"I said all good things!" The teenager deserved an Oscar for eavesdropping and Theo just shook his head as Reesa shrugged that it was just another thing he had to learn to love.

"Thank you for having me." Roger sat back in his seat as Billy Lou patted the one nearest her.

"Reesa, honey, sit. Theo's here now and can take over the cooking. Come visit."
"Any word from Jamie?" Theo asked.

"She's coming up the driveway." Clare pointed as she walked towards the deck and sat on the steps. She immediately hopped to her feet. "Oh, Teddy's here too." She took off at a jog to meet her friends and bring them around the side of the house.

"Teddy?" Roger asked.

"A friend from school," Reesa explained. "And Jamie owns the local coffee shop in town."

Roger watched as their friends rounded the house with warm welcomes and everyone fell into banter and conversation. Jamie, so excited to finally meet him, walked to him and gave him a hug that almost lifted him off his feet before she did the same to little Billy Lou. Reesa watched her friend bump Theo's hip and move him away from the food preparation and her hands went to work. Theo immediately fell into prepping the grill, everything seamlessly moving along with the slow movement of the sun as it began its descent behind the trees. Reesa reached out and tugged Clare's ponytail, her daughter's eyes sparkling up at her before she turned back to Teddy and looked at whatever he was showing her on his phone.

Life was good. Piney had delivered. And though she still had strides to make with her mother, her father sat on the porch and laughed with Billy Lou. Jamie and Theo bantered back and forth at the grill, and Clare and Teddy flirted with one another on the porch steps. Everyone was right where they should be. Everyone was happy. And so was she. Theo turned, his eyes narrowing in concern as he tried to gauge her temperament. His hands were covered in oil and spice as he prepared the meat to grill, but she walked over to him anyway and wrapped her arms around him. Pressing her head against his chest, she listened to the steady beat of his heart. "I'm good."

"I didn't ask," he stated, trying to look down at her face without using his dirty hands to adjust.

"But you were wondering," she whispered, finally meeting his eyes. "And I'm good." She smiled as she lifted on her tiptoes and kissed him. "And I love you, Theo." His brow wrinkled as he frowned at her and she giggled. "I know, you don't like the timing of my announcement, but I needed you to know."

Softening, he kissed her forehead. "I love you too."

Jamie gave a soft squeal of excitement next to them, but she kept her attention on the vegetables and her chopping. Reesa grinned at her friend before looking up at Theo again.

"Now, go away." Theo nodded towards her dad and Billy Lou. "Because I need to focus."

"Geez!" Reesa stepped away from him, their eyes lingering upon one another for a hot simmering second before she found a seat at the freshly painted patio table. Billy Lou reached over and squeezed her knee, giving her an encouraging wink before Reesa comfortably settled in her chair and soaked in her new life in Piney.

Continue the story with...

https://www.amazon.com/dp/B0BH4Z4D59

The Complete Siblings O'Rifcan Series Available in Paperback, Ebook, and Audiobook

Claron

https://www.amazon.com/dp/B07FYR44KX

Riley

https://www.amazon.com/dp/B07G2RBD8D

Layla

https://www.amazon.com/dp/B07HJRL67M

Chloe

https://www.amazon.com/dp/B07KB3HG6B

Murphy

https://www.amazon.com/dp/B07N4FCY8V

The Brothers of Hastings Ranch Series Available in Paperback, Ebook, and Audiobook

You can find the entire series here:
https://www.amazon.com/dp/B089LL1JJQ

All titles in The Lighthearted Collection Available in Paperback, Ebook, and Audiobook

Chicago's Best
https://www.amazon.com/dp/B06XH7Y3MF

Montgomery House
https://www.amazon.com/dp/B073T1SVCN

Beautiful Fury
https://www.amazon.com/dp/B07B527N57

McCarthy Road
https://www.amazon.com/dp/B08NF5HYJG

Blind Date
https://www.amazon.com/dp/B08TPRZ5ZN

**Check out the Epic Fantasy Adventure
Available in Paperback, Ebook, and
Audiobook**

U_{THE}NFADING
LANDS

The Unfading Lands
https://www.amazon.com/dp/B00VKWKPES

**Darkness Divided, Part Two in
The Unfading Lands Series**
https://www.amazon.com/dp/B015QFTAXG

**Redemption Rising, Part Three in
The Unfading Lands Series**
https://www.amazon.com/dp/B01G5NYSEO

AND DIAMONDY THE BAD GUY

Katharine and her five-year-old son released Captain Cornfield and Diamondy the Bad Guy in November 2021. This new books series launched with great success and has brought Katharine's career full circle and back to children's literature for a co-author partnership with her son. She loves working on Captain Cornfield adventures and looks forward to book two releasing in 2022.

Captain Cornfield and Diamondy the Bad Guy: The Great Diamond Heist, Book One

https://www.amazon.com/dp/1735812579

Subscribe to Katharine's Newsletter for news on upcoming releases and events!
https://www.katharinehamilton.com/subscribe.html

Find out more about Katharine and her works at:
www.katharinehamilton.com

Social Media is a great way to connect with Katharine. Check her out on the following:

Facebook: Katharine E. Hamilton
https://www.facebook.com/Katharine-E-Hamilton-282475125097433/

Twitter: @AuthorKatharine
Instagram: @AuthorKatharine

Contact Katharine:
khamiltonauthor@gmail.com

ABOUT THE AUTHOR

Katharine started to read through her former paragraph she had written for this section and almost fell asleep. She also, upon reading about each of her book releases and their stats, had completely forgotten about two books in her repertoire. So, she put a handy list of all her titles at the beginning of this book, for the reader, but mostly for her own sake. Katharine is also writing this paragraph in the third person... which is weird, so I'll stop.

I love writing. I've been writing since 2008. I've fallen in love with my characters and absolutely adore talking about them as if they're real people. They are in some ways, and they've connected with people all over the world. I'm so grateful for that. And I appreciate everyone who takes the time to read about them.

I could write my credentials, my stats, and all that jazz again, but quite frankly, I don't want to bore you. So, I'll just say that I'm happy. I live on the Texas Coast, (no ranch living for now), and I have two awesome little fellas (ages six and two) who keep me running... literally. Though I also say a lot of, "Don't touch that." "Put that back." "Stop pretending to bite your brother." "Did you just lick that?"

Thankfully, I have a dreamboat cowboy of a husband who helps wrangle them with me. I still have my sassy, geriatric chihuahua, Tulip. She may be slowing down a bit, but she will still bite your finger off if you dare try to touch her... the sweetheart. And then Paws... our loveable, snuggle bug, who thinks she is the size of a chihuahua, but is definitely not.

That's me in a nutshell.

Thank you for reading my work.

I appreciate each and every one of you.

Oh, and Claron has now sold over 100,000 copies. Booyah!

And Graham is not far behind him.... Woooooooo!

Made in the USA
Monee, IL
03 December 2024

72263999R00198